A Note from the Author

I know caves.

Do you know caves?

Caves streaked with minerals: green malachite, purple fluorite, blue john. Marbled walls of gypsum white and copper red. Earth's buried treasures.

Caves with clocks; elegant stalactites which slow-drip by slow-drip, inch their way through time. Caves with stalagmites, their ugly cousins. Lumpy, bumpy, mineral molehills.

Caves with thundering waterfalls, cascading torrents, flinging icy spray. Caves with tunnels which funnel swirling underground rivers. Rushing, twisting flumes, whooshing and swooshing, crashing and splashing.

Caves with secret, silent pools of crystal water. Like mirrored glass.

I know that ferns sometimes grow in caves. I have seen them.

And I know that damp, *cave* smell.

Do you?

www.rachaellindsay.com

Rachael Lindsay   2021

TALES FROM THE DARK HOLE:

A PIRATE'S PROMISE

Rachael Lindsay

TALES FROM THE DARK HOLE:

A PIRATE'S PROMISE

Nightingale Books

NIGHTINGALE PAPERBACK

A CIP catalogue record for this title is
available from the British Library.

ISBN 978 1 912021 01 7

Nightingale Books is an imprint of
Pegasus Elliot MacKenzie Publishers Ltd.
www.pegasuspublishers.com

First Published in 2019

Nightingale Books
Sheraton House Castle Park
Cambridge England

Printed & Bound in Great Britain

Dedication

For rapscallions and scallywags everywhere —
especially my second grandson,
Jacob Oliver,
with all Oma's love

xx

Acknowledgements

Once more, my special thanks and deep love to
Natalie Fern
for the illustrations in this book.
I know they will dance in the heads of children.

natalie.fern1@gmail.com

Once upon a gold doubloon…

Tobacco smoke curled lazily from her pipe, spiralling upwards in languid coils as she gazed out to sea. Her lace-trimmed shirt was undone at the throat, leaving her necktie to dangle and flutter in the cool breeze. Taking a swig of grog from her flagon and wiping her mouth with the back of one tattooed hand, she began to sing softly as her pi-rat sat, cleaning his fine whiskers:

"As I strolled by the seaside one mornin' so fair
To smell the salt water and breathe the sea air,
The waves they did call me, 'Come here and play!'
And I followed their siren, later that day.
And it's oh so long ago, and so, so far away,
And I'll sing m' sea shanty forever, they say."

Wooden crates and boxes were strewn on the sand around her, lids torn from their hinges, battered by wind and waves, their contents spilling out, glinting in the sunlight. For a greedy moment, the Sea Scoundrel considered them, head on one side, like a parrot about to squawk, 'Pieces of eight!' She saw the doubloons scattered carelessly, all polished and shining, their Spanish faces grinning. She saw the gold chains, crucifixes and pendants that had been ripped savagely from their owners, the clasps snapped and broken. She saw the rings that had been snatched from pleading, desperate fingers; the sparkling, silver brooches and beautiful, bronze bracelets torn from fair ladies; the fine goblets for fine wines; the buckles from belts, and daggers from dying men.

And there was an exquisite, jewelled dish, inlaid with gold and blood-red rubies which lay on its side, almost forgotten.

The treasures had been hard won. Piracy was a tough game, and many had paid the ultimate price — but the spoils were worth every man down.

Deep, deep down.

In

    the

        depths.

Bones on the sea bed now.

Picked clean by the nibblings of many tiny teeth.

"M' tailcoat is tattered, m' feet, they 'ave rot
But m' pipe is m' comfort and m' rat's m' mascot.
Old shipmates are long gone — for fish food, I think,
So, I'll raise m' old flagon and take me a drink.
And it's oh so long ago, and they're so far away,
And I'll sing m' sea shanty forever, they say."

Out on the horizon, there was the dark shadow of a sea-cave. It was small and tucked away, only just visible. The water around it was choppy. If she screwed her eyes up against the sun and stared hard enough, the Sea Crook could make out the white breakers on treacherous rocks. Her pi-rat perched on her knee, holding his ratty tail in one paw, and gazed out, too.

"What d' ye think, Romany?"

The pi-rat blinked and scratched a flea.

"D'ye reckon we can make it? Under the cover of darkness? A few trips, wi' m' sturdy boat, a favourable tide and fair weather?"

13

The pi-rat reflected for a moment. He twitched his pointy nose to sniff the direction of the wind and then looked up at his shipmate. Her cropped, curly hair was wild and ragged and caked in salt. Her single, hooped earring dangled and swung as she flashed him a wicked smile. He watched her take her pipe, tap the tobacco out onto a rock, and return her eyes to the water.

"Well, Romany? What d'ye think, eh?"

The rat dropped to the white sand, floofing it around him, like flour on a baker's board. He stood before the Sea Robber and returned her grin, all yellow teeth and whiskers.

"Romany Ratticus, the ruthless rodent, laughs in the face of wind and waves," he declared. "Romany Ratticus, the ruthless rodent, embraces excitement! Fetch the Jasmine Pearl, m'lady!"

Pulling on her swallow-tailed coat, she scooped him up and popped him niftily onto her shoulder. Her old boat was waiting.

"Let's go hide m' pretties then, Romany. Let's go!"

****

Twice upon a wave...

The *Jasmine Pearl* was resting on the beach, in the shade, quite close by. Although a little battered, she still had both oars and, despite the flaking paint and cracks in the wood, she was seaworthy enough.

She had saved a life, after all.

A few of the boxes, rammed heavy with pretties, were dragged across the sand and loaded on board. The Sea Scoundrel stood back, panting, and deliberated for a moment.

"How much weight d'ye think can she take, Romany?"

Scrambling eagerly onto the prow of the boat, her faithful pi-rat eyed up the booty. He pondered longer than usual, looking from one box to the next, chewing the end of a salty claw as he contemplated weight, waves and weather.

"Well, Romany? What d'ye think, eh?"

"Romany Ratticus, the ruthless rodent, feels a little wary, to be truthful, m'lady," he muttered, in reply. "Romany Ratticus, the ruthless rodent, thinks m'lady has loaded one crate too many for the *Jasmine Pearl* to handle."

He paused to assess the boat's contents further, still nibbling thoughtfully. "If m'lady removes just this one at the end, here," he continued, "Romany Ratticus would be a little more confident and the *Jasmine Pearl* would be a little more buoyant."

15

The last thing the Sea Crook wanted was to sink her valuable boat, full of even more valuable pretties, so out came the wooden box and the pi-rat nodded in approval. Eventually, the *Jasmine Pearl* was ready to sail. Putting her back against the craft and digging her boots into the sand, the lady robber heaved and shoved with all her strength until the sea lapped around her ankle-buckles and she could jump in. The tide was in their favour now and within minutes they were rowing at speed towards the sea-cave.

"M' crates they are loaded, the wind is set fair,
And I'll row till m' arms ache with never a care.
I'll get to that sea-cave and write out m' map,
To return for m' pretties without a mishap.
And it's oh so rocky — just feel the swell of the sea!
But we'll sing our sea shanty, m' rattie and me."

It was true. There was a swell. The sea became choppy and waves began to crash against the rocks. It became difficult to navigate the little boat safely between them, and Romany had to hold onto the side with both front paws, the wind blowing his whiskers hard back against his ears. He yelled directions to his lady as best he could, but the gale caught his words and tossed them into the spray.

It was a bumpy ride.

When the *Jasmine Pearl* finally came to rest, wedged between two sea boulders, the pi-rat breathed a sigh of relief, leapt out of the boat onto the shingle and secured its rope.

"Is m' rattie in one piece?" grinned the Sea Thief, shaking her wet curls and lifting the first crate. "'Twas a mite rough out there!"

"M'lady," Romany replied, with a certain degree of pride and fighting his feeling of sickness, "it takes more than a little sea swell to alarm Romany Ratticus, the ruthless rodent!" He grinned back at her and added, "Only dogs show fear, m'lady! Only dogs show fear!" And, so saying, he swaggered his way into the sea-cave.

Tunnels were found at the back of the main chamber. They had been worn away by ancient underground rivers and followed twists and turns, splitting into unexpected offshoots and opening out into surprise caverns and grottos. Once satisfied that they had disappeared far enough from the entrance, the crate was tucked under a shelf of overhanging rock and the two explorers made their way back to the boat. The next crate was lifted, carried through the maze of passageways, and concealed safely.

Then the next. And finally, the fourth.

On returning to an emptied *Jasmine Pearl*, a rough scroll of paper and a stub of charcoal was pulled from an inside pocket of the swallow-tailed coat. Licking the end of the makeshift pencil, by the light of the moon, a quick map of their secret route was drawn, in case they should forget when they made their next trip. The map was then slipped into a rocky cleft for safekeeping, just inside the sea-cave's entrance.

"How many more trips, eh?" she wondered, as she gazed back towards the distant beach where she had been washed up, a short time ago. "How many times back and forth?" Saying nothing to her faithful, furry friend but casting an experienced eye at the gathering storm clouds, Marnie McPhee began to row.

****

Thrice-a-rowing to and fro…

Romany, too, had seen the mushrooming clouds and had spent enough time on board ships to know the sky was threatening danger. He watched Marnie cram the last of the crates and boxes into a creaking *Jasmine Pearl*, as he twiddled his ratty tail, thoughtfully, in his scrawny paws. Was she loading too many? A chilly breeze had begun to blow stinging grains of sand across the beach, and the waves, which had been mere ripples running up the shoreline, began to slap against the side of the boat spitting salty foam into the air.

"Wind's gettin' up a bit," Marnie commented, at last. "We'd best be on our way if we're goin' to make it to the cave afore the storm sets in. P'raps have to spend the night there, m' rattie, if the tide turns against us. I've got us some hardtack and m' grog, so we'll not be a-starvin' or a-dyin' of thirst."

The pi-rat shifted from one thin foot to the other, rocking from side to side as he studied the distance they would have to row, once more. It wasn't ship biscuits or rum that concerned him.

"If I might be so bold, m'lady," he ventured. "The *Jasmine Pearl* does look a tad overloaded again. Do you think we really need *all* of it?"

Marnie wiped her brow with the back of her tattooed hand and took her clay pipe out of her top pocket. Then, clamping it firmly between her teeth, she reached into another pocket for her tobacco and, after unrolling the linen in which it was wrapped, proceeded to stuff the bowl. She took a few minutes to do this thoroughly, packing it down and staring out to sea now and then, lost in thought. Once lit, she took a couple of deep sucks on the stem and finally, breathing out smoke, she sang:

"I'll hide m' sweet pretties in yonder dark cave,
'Cos I promised m' maties their treasures I'd save.
The waves they may smite me and carry me down,
But I'll row wi' m' treasures, e'en though I may drown.
And it's oh so blust'ry, and the cave's so far away,
And I'll sing m' sea shanty forever, they say."

The pi-rat understood completely. The boat might be groaning with the weight of this last load, the sea-cave might be a considerable distance away and the sky might be full of dark warning, but she had promised. A *promise* was a *promise* and should *never* be broken.

Even amongst pirates.

Especially amongst pirates.

Loyalty and honour were part of the pirates' code. Honour amongst thieves, it was true, but nevertheless, honour. It was a poor pirate who did not stand by his fellow shipmates. This treasure had belonged to *all* of them. They had fought hard for it against their fearsome foes, the surging seas and the wicked wiles of weather, and each had vowed to safeguard it for all. In the end, it was the weather and waves that had almost won, had it not been for Marnie McPhee and the pint-sized *Jasmine*

Pearl. They had been a formidable team — and Marnie was not going to let the weather beat her now; her oath to keep the plunder safe, was one she had made with a true pirate's heart. When the others had perished, unable to keep their boots on the rolling deck, pitching overboard one by one, screaming into the ocean's maw, she had held onto the helm, steering the mother vessel towards land. When flung from the ship's wheel, she had clung onto wet ropes, blistering and ripping the skin on her hands as she was tossed like a rag doll against the masts. When, finally, there was a giant groan and an ear-splitting crack from the belly of the ship, she knew she had only one chance left. *The Jasmine Pearl*.

The little, half-broken rowing boat was swinging from a single tied rope, which was frayed and at snapping point. With a swipe of her dagger, the rope was cut and the *Jasmine Pearl* splashed into the water below. Marnie had taken one last look at the great ship with ripped, black sails, which had been her home for the last few years and then hurled herself off the bulwark, crashing into the waves which covered her head and dragged her down. From below the surface of the water, she could just make out the hull of the *Jasmine Pearl*. Her one chance. With fierce determination and single-minded strength, she had forced herself to the surface and grappled with the side of the little boat. Heaving herself up and tumbling onto the deck, she had proceeded to battle valiantly, against all odds, to reach the shore.

Marnie McPhee had been the sole survivor — apart from a bedraggled Romany, who having jumped ship to join her, washed up on the beach exactly like a drowned rat, alongside the treasures from the pirate ship.

And now, she had a promise to keep.

The clay pipe was emptied against a rock and the Sea Robber picked up her companion, holding him aloft in front of her. "One last trip, eh, Romany? Are ye up for it?"

"Romany Ratticus, the ruthless rodent, is at your service, m'lady!" He fell from her grip onto the sand. "Though the wind may blow my whiskers and the rain may soak my fur, we'll ride the surf together like true pirates of the sea! Weigh the anchor and hoist the mizzen m'lady! Romany Ratticus is by your side!"

And with that, he leapt once more into the loaded *Jasmine Pearl*.

****

Forth, my pretties to save…

The *Jasmine Pearl* struggled. Battered as she had been by her original casting off from the black-sailed mother ship into a raging ocean, and then weakened further by her trips to and from the sea-cave, she was taking in water now, at an alarming rate. Romany Ratticus stood at the prow once more, braving the salty slaps which doused his fine whiskers, shouting encouragement to Marnie who fought to keep the craft in a straight line. He was more than a little concerned. As ruthless and courageous as he might have felt, this didn't look good, and both of them knew it. It had been reckless to set sail this last time with the little boat overloaded and the weather set ferociously against them.

Soon, they reached a point where there was no turning back. They were committed to their fate.

Marnie battled against the surf which rolled and churned around them. The oars became too hefty to pull on, the waves dragging them from the *Jasmine Pearl* as Marnie's muscles burned with pain. Getting the blades to rise out of the water for another stroke was impossible, but she held on to the precious wooden paddles, wet hair matted against her face and shouted out to the pelting sky:

"NOW, I DON'T WANT NO TEARS
NOR A HALO, NOT ME,

JUST GIVE ME STRONG ARMS,
AND I'LL CONQUER THE SEA!
I'LL SAIL TO THAT CAVE,
NO MATTER THE PAIN —
WITH M'RATTIE BESIDE ME,
I'LL NOT BATTLE IN VAIN!"

The pi-rat released his tight-clawed grip on the *Jasmine Pearl* and turned to face the Sea Scoundrel as she cried out in defiance:

"I WILL RETURN! I'LL FOLLOW M'MAP AND *NEVER* GIVE UP M'PRETTIES!"

She looked wild and furious and bold with her head turned proudly up to the heavens and her eyes, closed. He had never seen her look so unflinching — or so beautiful.

"ROMANY RATTICUS, THE RUTHLESS RODENT IS BY YOUR SIDE, M'LADY!" he yelled, springing into her lap.

Together, they sang out as stridently as they could:
"And it's oh so long ago…"
Water.
"And so, so far away…"
Up noses.
"And I'll sing m' sea shanty…"
In mouths.
"Forever, they say!"
Swallowing.
Gulping.
Choking.

Hands and paws grappling.

Holding onto each other.

"And I'll sing m' sea shanty forever, they say…"

    Down.

        Deep down.

            Deep down…

                … into

                    the

                        depths.

****

Chapter One
Eggs

Spring was in the air. It had arrived with a gentle, warm breeze and a clear, bluebell sky. Leaf buds had unfurled at last and the trees and hedgerows seemed to have burst into bright green clothing, overnight. The birds rejoiced. Twitters and tweets, chirrups and chatters were to be heard at dawn and dusk. The flowers began to peep out from their sepal beds, sleepily opening their eyes and throwing open their petals, like discarded bedclothes. Egg yolk yellows, pristine purples and forget-me-not blues. Everything was young and fresh and new.

Hobnail was sweeping. Furiously. She had her trusty besom clasped tightly in her six-fingered hands as clouds of grime and smut billowed around her. For a brief moment, she paused in her work and leant against the brush, thinking how much more fun it would be to be whizzing along bouncy paths on her wheel-cycle, feeling the wind in her hair and the chill on her face. "Ashes is so pesky being!" she complained aloud, to nobody in particular, watching the grey air settle slowly, covering everything around her, once more.

The broken door to her tumbledown cottage swung on its single hinge, allowing the sunbeams to highlight the swirls of dust, still dancing. She sighed loudly and shook her head. She had worked so hard this morning, and how her hunched back ached! She had risen early, even before the birds were in full voice, and dragged her old sofa outside, where she had bashed and beaten it with a plastic fly-swatter, trying her hardest to shift the soot and dirt from its worn covers. She had removed the long stems of mugwort from the smouldering fire and stacked them in a corner, before splooshing rainwater over the charred sticks and faintly glowing embers, in an attempt to damp it down properly. She had crabbed her way down the cellar steps and tidied the crates and boxes which stored fallen autumn apples and jars of woodlouse jam. She had cleaned and sorted, and sorted and cleaned, and there were definitely no rats or mice or spiders anywhere.

And now, despite being tidier, her home was *still* grubby.

"I's not particularly enjoying this springtime work, Dear Ones," she grumbled, looking across to Warty Toad and Snidey Slug. "And I am noticing that you is both not being of any helpfulness!"

The toad blinked languidly at the slug. The slug waggled his eye stalks back. Both sort of shrugged, in a toady and sluggy sort of fashion. Help? What did she expect them to do? Much as they loved their mistress, there really was a limit. Neither could sweep, nor could they move boxes and crates or mouldy sofas. They could no more deal with the ashes from the fire, than they could dust or polish. Apart from keeping an eye out for tasty spider gobblings, should Hobnail have missed any, the best thing they thought they *could* do, was to keep out of the way — they certainly didn't fancy being swept up in a rare flurry of housework. As it was, wherever they tried to go,

27

the broom seemed to follow them, sending Warty Toad plip-plopping quickly to side-step the twigs, and causing Snidey Slug to sneeze snottily from all the dust.

Tutting loudly and muttering under her breath, Hobnail propped her brush up against a crumbling pile of bricks which had once been a dividing wall and left the cleaning behind her. Fresh air beckoned and she could resist it no longer. She tried to straighten her shoulders as she stood in the spring sunshine, her single working eye blinking in the bright light; her greyed-out, blind eye calm today, needing no plotting or planning, for all was well.

Lucy-fur, the ginger cat, had found a warm, snoozy spot and stretched out lazily, without a care in the world, ignoring the feathery hens which clucked and pecked in the grit around her. Despite the morning's frustrations, Hobnail had to smile at the soft fluffiness of her pet.

"It is seeming to me that *nobody* else is having working in mind, this morning!" she commented, bending down to stroke the ginger fur, with twelve knobbly fingers. "You just stays there, my pretty-prooper, and find joyfulness in sunny times and moments. All the mousey-pests are scurry-gone in any case, so you is having very little else to be doing, after all."

It was true. Although Hobnail had checked the cellar for mice and rats, she was confident there would be none. Lucy-fur was a ferocious hunter and prowled menacingly each night to keep the dwelling clear of vermin. She enjoyed pest control and was an Expert Pest Controller. The cat purred loudly, plucking at the warm air with sharp claws, a curly grin on her face and whiskers, before rolling over and promptly falling back to sleep.

****

Hobnail was not really cross. She loved her Dear Ones as if they were her children. They were her only friends, cast out as she had been, for being different, ugly and disfigured. She had lived a troubled childhood and, apart from her aged Great Aunt, Tabitha Wrinklewarts, who showed her how to sow seeds, grow and use strange plants and herbs, nobody cared for her and so she inhabited her tumbledown cottage, a long way from others, where she could be left alone. Occasionally, Hobnail would venture into the town — to beg for something vital, perhaps, or to scavenge in a bin — but, more often than not, she kept herself to herself. She knew she was not popular with the townspeople. It had always been so. After all, hadn't even her own mother rejected the odd-looking child she had borne? People did not trust her and were afraid of her appearance, showing heartlessness in their cruel treatment of her. This, Hobnail bore with weary resignation some of the time; at other times, she did not, for when she was sufficiently provoked, she would exact a vengeful punishment, using a combination of strange incantations and peculiar ingredients, collected from her *special place*.

This *special place* was a secret retreat, deep in the forest, where the trees were no longer oak and ash and beech and birch. It was a place well past the dogwood and elder, the hazel and the juniper, the rowan and the yew. It was a place where the long, green, slime fronds would drip and

drop and

30

       dribble and

         drobble.

Hobnail had discovered this damp hideaway whilst wandering one day, and although told to leave, she had found it to be a rich source of supplies for her hexes: swamp tree bark, bird talons, bat droppings, red and black beetles, wood lice and butterfly wings. Strange plants grew there, too. The strange plants she required from time to time. *'Know your poisons!'* she had been told, many years before.

And she did.

Her sanctuary under the long green, slime fronds, was the Dark Hole. This was where Hobnail hid her strange findings, in bottles and jars and boxes, and it was where she stayed now and then, especially if she were to be cooking up some revenge in her old, copper pot. Great Boulder watched over the entrance and would never allow access to anyone but its mistress. This extraordinary rock had started life as a pebble on a beach, but immediately Hobnail saw its potential and had transformed it into a boulder of great weight and importance. It was now a perfect front door for the Dark Hole and, although somewhat stubborn and lazy, showed fierce loyalty and devotion: a true guard dog of a boulder.

   However, there were enemies under the long, green, slime fronds. It was a dingy and sinister place, and Hobnail had to be wary. Whenever she left the fresh air and sunshine hours of her tumbledown cottage, she entered an altogether different world. She was not wanted there. She was not welcome. The Leaf Man, Liar-nel, did not like Hobnail; this was *his* domain and he wanted to keep her *out*. His leaflette friends, Fiblet and Fibkin, dangled from his twiggy fingers as he watched her come and go, staying hidden whilst hatching his plans. He camouflaged himself against the bark of the swamp trees and waited for news. He was always well-informed of her movements. He had his spies. The Moss-makers *clack-clack-clacked* as they knitted and crocheted with busy fingers, passing their messages on from one to the other, burbling with squashy lips. The two Mushrumps were dedicated in their determination to find facts — although often a little late with their information, as they spent much time checking and re-checking with each other, in case they had made a mistake.

"Are you sure what you know, Mrs. Mushrump?"

"Well, I can't be *sure*, Mr. Mushrump, but I *think*..."

"You think *what*, Mrs. Mushrump? What is it you are thinking? You have to be *sure*, you know."

"I *know*, Mr. Mushrump. I know I have to be sure, but I can't be sure what I know is for *sure*, you know…"

And then there was Crow-cus.

Crow-cus flew on silent, black wings, by day and night. He would perch and listen, never missing a trick. *Crauk! Crauk!*

The Leaf Man had made himself quite clear. He had challenged Hobnail, making her feel ill at ease and sometimes frightened. But she would *not* be bullied. She ignored Liar-nel with a grim determination, much to his exasperation, and she continued to visit the place under the long, green, slime fronds whenever she wanted to. The Leaf Man drummed his twiggy

32

fingers, narrowed his eyes and kept his knowing smile. He would do anything he could to get rid of this nuisance old crone, with hunched back, twelve fingers, blind eye and heavy boots.

****

The clucking and pecking hens had laid some beautiful eggs. They were white-shelled, warm and so fresh! There were only three, and they were only small, but Hobnail was delighted and very excited at the prospect of a tasty meal later in the day. Her meals were usually put together from foraged or scavenged scraps. Squirrels and mice made good stew, but were very tricky to catch, and those she found lying in her rutted lane were frequently half-eaten already and somewhat maggoty; bins in the town were often overflowing with discarded food, but it was not always to her taste, even though Hobnail understood that anything was better than nothing. So, eggs! A wonderful treat! Her hens were not young chickens any more and rarely laid eggs nowadays, but there must have been something in the spring air this particular morning. There they were, nestled in some straw in an old apple box at the side of the cottage. Twelve gentle fingers picked them up and cradled them, taking every care not to crack the pearly shells. They were carried into the dilapidated cottage and placed tenderly into a chipped, pottery bowl.

"Eggsies for tea!" Hobnail told Warty Toad and Snidey Slug, her yellow teeth grinning widely. "We is having a delicious feast of yummy-ness, this evening! Eggsies and leaves of the dandelion!" Her mouth watered at the prospect.

****

Having decided enough was enough when it came to cleaning, and having her meal all planned, Hobnail gathered up Warty Toad and Snidey Slug. There was a job to do, of great importance, and she needed their assistance. A quick glance in her old, cracked mirror confirmed it. After all her hard work, her hair was dusty, cobwebby and in need of damson dye. Hobnail was not at all vain — indeed, she had little to be vain about — but, her one indulgence was her hair colour. It also meant that she had the perfect excuse to pop her Dear Ones into her bicycle basket and jump on, at last!

"Come now, dearies. I is in needs of being plum-colourated and I is wanting of your helpfulness, if you please so! Let us be wheel-cycling and beetle-squashing."

So saying, she took them outside to her battered bicycle, which was leaning up against a crumbling, stone wall. Soon, two heavy, black hobnail boots pushed down hard on the pedals and the three were whizzing along the wobbly lane to the edge of the forest. Warty Toad and Snidey Slug were well-used to travelling in Hobnail's bicycle basket. They were used to clinging on through the jumps and jolts. They were used to the occasional bruise and knock. They were used to the bouncing and bumping. They never arrived at their destination without feeling a little queasy though, and today was no different. It was with considerable relief that they plopped and slithered out of their wicker carriage, to wait dutifully at their mistress's feet. The bicycle was left behind them, hidden from view in the undergrowth, and the little troop were soon under the long, green, slime fronds which dripped and

       dropped and

           dribbled and

               drobbled onto their heads.

****

A murmuring began in the mossy marshes. A mumbling and a whispering. Squashy, wet lips passed a message on from this green clump to that green clump; from one wet mat to the next. *Clack! Clack! Clack!*

****

Fortunately, although Warty Toad thoroughly enjoyed the pulping of red and black beetles to make Hobnail's hair dye, there was one bottle of pokeweed berry cordial left from the autumn brewing. This would save considerable time, as finding the right number of beetles was always hard work and then it was always tricky to get the right ratio to blend into the exact colour required. The three had entered the Dark Hole by the usual method: a tappity-tap on Great Boulder with a small stone, then a slither and a slide from one, a hop and plop from the next, and a cautious lowering over the side from the last,

35

before all were settled safely inside their special place. Great Boulder grumbled a little, as usual, when asked to roll back to keep them hidden, but it did so, knowing all too well that its mistress would not be happy if it made too much noise. Glow worms, in their glass bottles, were shaken gently and the Dark Hole was lit in all colours, blinking and winking as they shuffled about.

"We is lucky indeed to be finding a bottle of cordial, my dears," Hobnail commented, lifting the precious dye from a ledge on the Forbidden Wall. "That is meaning we can be quick-stickery and chip-choppery in my hair colouration. Then we wheel-cycles home in no times, for eggsies! Bring me my shell dish, if you please so."

Warty and Snidey knew just what to do; this was a familiar routine to them. In no time, they had dragged and pushed their mistress's prized dish over to her. The syrupy pokeweed berry juice was poured in and swirled around so that it coated the beautiful shell. This dish was the only really pretty object that Hobnail owned. Found on the beach one day, it had been polished until it shone in mother-of-pearl shimmers, and it had been her exquisite treasure ever since. Now, it was lifted carefully, in the gnarled six fingers of one hand, the syrup poured onto her foggy hair, whilst the other hand scrunched and crumpled it through. A quick flick was all that was needed, showering the Dark Hole in plum droplets, and Hobnail was transformed. She grinned at her Dear Ones, her yellow teeth shining in the glow worms' light, her greyed-out eye crinkling at the corners in satisfaction. "We is done," she announced.

****

Outside, the Mushrumps had been watching.

"Just the usual, I would say, Mrs. Mushrump, wouldn't you?"

"It's hard to say, Mr. Mushrump. Hard to say."

"Why is it *'hard to say'*, Mrs. Mushrump? You've seen what *I've* seen. You've heard what *I've* heard. Why is it *'hard to say'*?"

"Well, we don't really know what she *did* down there, do we, Mr. Mushrump? We saw her go in with toad and slug, and we saw her come out again — but we don't really know what she *did*, do we, Mr. Mushrump?"

"I suppose you might have a point, Mrs. Mushrump. You might have a point. But she wasn't there long, was she? So, she can't have done much, Mrs. Mushrump."

"Like I say, it's hard to say, Mr. Mushrump. It's hard to say."

****

Hobnail reached her tumbledown cottage, full of eager hunger, a clutch of freshly-picked dandelion leaves in her overcoat pocket and a scrummy plan for tea. However, on entering her home, her excitement evaporated.

The chipped, pottery bowl lay on its side, on the floor. Each of the three eggs was broken open, the shells gnawed, and the contents gone.

And something was not quite right with Lucy-fur. She was prowling, lashing her tail and sniffing the air. It was clear she could smell something odd.

****

Chapter Two
Shells

Without doubt, teatime had been a great disappointment. The empty, broken eggshells had been ground underfoot with a frustrated hobnail boot and the dandelion leaves had been made into a thin, watery, green soup. Everybody's tummy rumbled. Warty Toad decided to go on a spider hunt, hoping that the earlier spring cleaning had not got rid of *all* creepy crawlies, and Snidey Slug sucked in vain on his bottom lip until it was quite swollen and made his sulky pout even more noticeable. Their mistress had stomped about the dilapidated cottage with a black cloud above her head.

"All I is wanting is eggsies," she muttered. "Good, tasty, filling eggsies treat. Eggsies from *my* chucks. Eggsies fresh laid and new. Eggsies I am being of carefulness with, to save for *my* tea!" She glowered at the broken door. "I must be fixing of that hinge — and when I is finding out who is guilty of egg-thievery, I is fixing of them also!"

The two Dear Ones kept quiet. They both knew that there was never any point in trying to talk to Hobnail when she was in a temper. They both knew they should keep out of the way and wait for the storm to pass. Happily, Warty had found a couple of small spiders to squash at the back of his mouth with a satisfying 'pop' and had taken great pleasure in flicking the thin, tickly legs around his tongue. No doubt, in a day or two, there would be more tasty delights for his entertainment and satisfaction.

Lucy-fur had taken herself outside to find field mice for her tea. There hadn't been enough eggs for all of them anyway and she had scarpered when Hobnail had started stomping, afraid her beautiful, ginger tail would be trodden on. There were plenty of hidey-holes for small furry creatures in the meadows and hedgerows around the cottage, and when she had eaten her fill of crunchy bones and warm, juicy inside bits, she spent a few skittish moments finding others to play shuttlecock with. By the time she poked her inquisitive nose around the door, about an hour later, her mistress was calmer and admiring her damson hair in the old, cracked mirror.

"Eggsies or no eggsies, I is pleased-feeling with my hair, Dear Ones," she declared. She crumpled it untidily with her grimy fingers and then drew out a black patch from an overcoat pocket, carefully positioning it over her greyed-out eye. "I is looking quite the business!"

Warty Toad and Snidey Slug considered their mistress from a distance. All of her. From her eye patch and damson hair, to her hunched back, dirty overcoat and twelve bent fingers, she was, in their eyes, truly splendid.

"Time is marching towards a bedtime story, dearies. Come sit with me quick-stickery and I shall begin."

This was more like it! Warty and Snidey were great fans of bedtime stories and Hobnail was a great storyteller. There wasn't always time for them to get together like this, but whenever the chance arose, whether in the old cottage or the Dark Hole, it was grabbed eagerly with all fingers and toes. As they slimily-slid and plip-plopped to their favourite places, one, on Hobnail's bony shoulder, the other, nestled under a damp, hairy armpit, the Dear Ones knew story time wasn't just about the story; it was about *togetherness*. It was about the comfort of all of them being snuggled up on the mouldy sofa, having a cuddle. The stories were usually about Hobnail's own life and things that had happened to her; she had never had story books as a child, and so these tales were the best way to entertain her Dear Ones and to tell them something of herself. Lucy-fur jumped onto Hobnail's lap and turned around this way, and then changed her mind and turned around the other way, and then decided *that* way wasn't *quite* right and the first way was best, licked her fur briefly with the tip of her pretty, pink tongue, purred for a moment, and then curled herself up into a ball of ginger and white fluff.

"My shell dish," Hobnail began. "Is being a thing of great beautifulness."

This Warty Toad and Snidey Slug knew only too well. They had used it many times to colour Hobnail's hair. Snidey slithered from his mistress's shoulder to her neck and almost purred into her ear.

"It is beautiful, Mistress. Just like you."

Warty Toad rolled his poppy eyes and grimaced. Always point scoring, that ghastly gastropod. He felt slightly sick. Hobnail smiled in the gathering dusk and petted the slug, stroking her long fingernail down his back, making him dip and arch his soft body in appreciation. "I is of a mind to be telling you both about my beautiful dish of shell," she whispered. At this, they both settled and listened attentively. "Flotsam and jetsam, my Dear Ones," Hobnail began. "Is always good funnery to find flotsam and jetsam."

****

For a long time now, Hobnail had enjoyed trips to the windswept beach at the bottom of the rugged cliffs which could be scaled only by means of a winding, treacherous path made up of gritty stones. The path was narrow and hidden from view and so it was ideal for her; she never wanted to be seen or challenged or spoken to. It was a short bicycle trip away from her home, which took her through the local fields, past the badger setts and over wild moorland which was good merely for grazing sheep who didn't mind the dry, stubby grass and the cold breeze from the sea. Her battered bicycle was always concealed well amongst the gorse bushes and there it waited, with empty basket, for her return; it was her trusty steed.

Flotsam, the debris in water that had been the result of a sinking boat or ship, was a rare find. Occasionally, a trinket would be spotted, washed up amongst the seaweed and shale, or trapped in between the rocks, crabs sidling over it, suspiciously. Hobnail had found an odd spoon or two, which had been useful, and once she had come across a fisherman's hipflask, which contained a foul-tasting liquor but, once emptied and rinsed, made a convenient receptacle for rose hip cordial, of which she was particularly fond. She had never

42

found anything of any great value, but it was always fun to search and find useful items, now and then. Officially, any items of worth could be reclaimed by their owner, if they hadn't drowned at sea, so it was just as well Hobnail had little to show for her beach combing — she would not have liked to have been accused of theft.

Jetsam, however, was another matter. If anything had been thrown *deliberately* overboard by the crew of a ship, usually in distress, it would be hers to keep. Quite how she was to know the difference between flotsam and jetsam, Hobnail was not sure, but she liked to muse on the history of the things she found, their owners and the stories behind them. If she hid her findings carefully, no one would know, anyway. She was a great believer in: '*Finders, keepers, losers, weepers,*' and thought people should look after their property with more care, if they didn't want her to come across it.

****

Warty Toad shuffled a little under Hobnail's armpit. He wasn't altogether sure he cared about the rules of flotsam and jetsam. "But what about the shell dish, Mistress?" he interrupted in a muffled voice. "Shells don't belong to anyone, do they? They just belong to the sea, don't they?"

"You is right talking, Warty," replied Hobnail. "Shells is of natural origins. Man can't make such wondrous things of wonder! Peoples should always be appreciating Lady Nature and all she is offering us."

Lucy-fur sat up unexpectedly, her paws pressing into Hobnail's knees. She thought she had heard a scratching sound. Her ears were alerted to the cellar door but, even though she stared with her best saucer eyes, there was nothing to be seen. Her tail flicked ever so slightly. A calming hand stroked her, and she settled down again, but she kept one wary eye open.

****

Hobnail had always loved picking up shells. She turned each one over in her six-fingered hands and pondered about the animal whose home it had been. It was a constant source of amazement to her that a small, slimy creature should make its own protective outer layer with salt and minerals from its food and surroundings. How marvellous was nature that these vulnerable, fragile bodies could be wrapped up in a hard shell, safe from predators and the elements? She paused in her talking for a minute to reflect on this. There had been times in her own, sad life, when she would have felt much safer enfolded in a shell. She could have wrapped herself up inside and not been hurt by the jibes and sneers she had suffered, just because she was different. She could have been sealed off from danger and threats. It had been difficult to live away from other people, shunned as she had been because of her disfigured back, blind eye and twelve fingers. Hobnail smiled a little bitterly in the gloom of the shabby room.

"I don't need a shell to keep me safe," Snidey whispered in the gathering darkness. "And I like being squishy."

44

"You is not needing a shell, Snidey-pet, because I is keeping you safes. We all is keeping each other safes."

Warty, not wishing to be left out of the general chat of things, was just about to add a comment about slugs being revolting in their squishiness, when Lucy-fur pricked up her ears once more and this time, growled. Another scritch-scratch? And now, there was a really strong smell of mouse…

****

So, having such a love of shells, when Hobnail came across a shell dish, full of silt and sand, washed up and discarded on the beach, she was immediately thrilled. It was not just a simple shell. It had been shaped and fashioned into a bowl, with a narrow lip at one end to pour from. Whether it was flotsam or jetsam, she neither knew, nor cared. This dish was going to be hers, no matter what the history behind it! For a few minutes, she knelt on the beach, gazing at the wonder of nature in her hands. Perhaps it had come from a distant land — underneath the salt and sandy coating, she could see a marbling of different colours, perhaps made from exotic plants and crystals which its creator had eaten. Perhaps it had been shaped by the grinding of sand once the creature had left it behind. Perhaps it had been tossed under and over waves for miles and miles and miles. Hobnail felt the lip of the dish with the tip of her finger. Had this part been an entrance or exit for the animal which used to live in it? Or had it been formed by human hand, someone with a special file and time to treasure and fashion it into a part to pour from? And if so, who? What did the dish once hold? How many hands had poured from it? The beachcomber smiled to herself. There was no doubt about it. Here, in her wizened hands, was a thing of nature, of beauty and of times gone by!

****

Was that the tip of a tail, over there, by the cellar door? Lucy-fur, tail flicking, stared fixedly into the shadows. She thought the cellar had been checked and swept out, but perhaps some more expert pest controlling was needed. Noiselessly, the cat flattened back her ears and slunk off Hobnail's lap, keeping her profile low so that her tummy almost touched the old slates on the floor. The mouse smell was even stronger now and Lucy-fur decided that it was not mouse at all… but *rat*.

****

The beach that day happened to be festooned with seaweed. This was exactly what Hobnail needed. Placing her precious find carefully onto a nearby rock, she darted here and there, gathering a strange bouquet of sea lettuce, sponge weed, sea horsetail, straggle weed, wart weed and bladder wrack. Each seaweed type was chosen for its colour and texture, and all were stuffed into her overcoat pockets.

"Mermaids' purses is being needed, also," she whispered to herself, in a fever of excitement. "I must be finding of shark egg cases! Where is they, I wonders?"

A further scouring of the area located a couple of empty pouches close by, up on the strandline. These were seized with eager fingers and also thrust into an overcoat pocket.

Hobnail scanned the beach. All was as quiet as usual. There was nobody there to witness her activity or to spot her picking up the shell dish, ready to scurry to her sea-cave, but it was better to be cautious and so the dish was tucked under her coat and clutched tightly in the folds of the fabric, hidden and protected, just like its occupier had once been, long ago.

****

"But your shell dish is kept in the Dark Hole, Mistress," interrupted Warty Toad, creeping out from his armpit nest. "Why did you take it to the sea-cave? Why didn't you just pop it into your bicycle basket and hurry to the long, green, slime fronds?"

Hobnail put a grimy finger to her hairy lips to shush him. "I is taking the beautiful preciousness to my whirlpool, of course." This did not really answer Warty's question. He had never been to the sea-cave and he had never seen a whirlpool. His toady adventures had been limited to the nearby lanes and hedgerows, the drip,

drop,

dribble,

drobble,

of the long, green, slime fronds and, only on the odd occasion, the beach itself. He had never been able to cross the water to the sea-cave where Hobnail occasionally spent her time and

47

she had never offered to take him as she always wanted to be there alone. He had no idea what a whirlpool was or why his mistress should take the shell dish there. He was just taking a breath to ask further questions, his curiosity aroused — when Lucy-fur, ginger tail lashing, made a sudden *pounce!*

They all looked over to the cellar door.

"Lucy-fur? Is you up to mouse-catchery, my dear?" Hobnail called out. "I is of certain mindedness that no mousies remain in the cellar. Come back to my lap and be of calm in nature."

The little cat did not move. She sat by the cellar door and kept watch. The tip of a thin tail was nowhere to be seen now, but she was sure it had been there.

****

The whirlpool swirled and spiralled. Its churning was fascinating and strangely hypnotic. Hobnail watched the water disappearing down into the depths of its dizzying plughole, recognising the giddy effect it had on her. She had discovered it many years before when exploring some parts of the sea-cave for the first time. Her boots had led her steadfastly over the rocks and stones of the secret tunnels, taking different turns, following the distant sound of falling water. Her greyed-out eye, always ready for plotting and planning, had memorised the route well, making its own blind map in her head. She knew she would be able to return by closing her good eye and letting the blind one take charge without hesitation, having remembered the number of steps to the right or left, up or down, over or around obstacles with ease. The noise of water had gradually become louder and louder and when, eventually, Hobnail had come across an underground waterfall, the thundering tumult had delighted and excited her. Icy water sprayed her face, scattering droplets in her hair. As it cascaded downwards, her coat became soaked and she became drenched.

And, at the base of the waterfall had been the whirlpool.

It was mesmerising.

Clefts and fissures in the rocky ceiling allowed just enough light to be able to make out the whirling spiral as it took the water spinning away beneath the cave floor.

Hobnail's breath had been taken away with it.

Now, deep in the cave once more, she gasped again at the sight. She laughed out loud at the waterfall's spit and licked her fingers, wet from wiping the water from her face. Tentatively, she stretched out, shell dish in hand and allowed the splashings to wash and rinse it thoroughly. Gone was the salty seawater and the fine layer of silt. Crouching low, she placed the dish carefully on the rocks and took out handfuls of seaweed from her overcoat pockets. She rubbed and polished, and polished and rubbed, binding and blending magic minerals. Gradually, deep sea-colours began to emerge. The mermaids' purses were filled with waterfall water to pour into it, for a final sluice, and at last the shell dish was ready.

Perfection.

In the depths of those tunnels, in front of the whirlpool's roar, Hobnail held her most precious find.

****

Warty Toad and Snidey Slug were entranced. They had been given a glimpse of the sea-cave's secrets. Their heads were full

50

of waterfall splashes and whirlpool circles. When they closed their eyes, they could imagine the seaweed being scrubbed around the precious shell dish and Hobnail's twelve fingers collecting water in the mermaids' purses.

"That's amazing, Mistress!" declared Warty. "Will you tell us more about the sea-cave? Please?"

Hobnail nodded. Her story was not quite finished.

Snidey slipped from her neck to perch on her shoulder once more. "But how did you get the shell dish into the Dark Hole without You-Know-Who seeing?"

"Ah, my dearie. Liar-nel is not knowing abouts my dish of beauty! I takes every care on my homewards journeyings," winked the storyteller. "I has my ways through tunnels, you sees. I has my ways."

"Ways?" Snidey queried. "Which 'ways'?"

"Ways and means, my dear. Ways and means." Hobnail smiled mysteriously. She pulled her eye patch away from her face and gave them a slow wink. "There is being a secret tunnel," she continued, her voice soft and low. "A secret tunnel from the sea-cave, which twisterates to the Dark Hole. Right through the underground rocks she goes..." The Dear Ones looked at each other in astonishment. "She is opening up at the bottom of the Forbidden Wall where I keeps my special-lovelies. She is being my escape route and my sea-cave connection, if you likes." Their mistress paused. "In case I is needings of her."

A sudden yellow-toothed yawn.

And a warty-lipped one.

And another slimy-slobbery one.

It was time for them all to sleep and so they settled down for the night.

Except for Lucy-fur.

The little cat was sure she could hear the curious sound of whiskery snoring coming from underneath the old sofa.

****

Chapter Three
Footprints

Ting, ting! A bent bicycle, pedalled by two black boots, bumped and rattled its way over the rough ground to the cliffs, then Hobnail made her way down the narrow, shale path to the beach. All were on a hunt for spiny sea hedgehogs, delicious treats which were to be found, occasionally, washed up in the kelp. Hobnail had stirred early that morning, with pangs of hunger gnawing at her empty belly and, just as she was about to grumble once more about broken eggs, her third, future-telling eye had woken up. This secret, inner eye had foretold the tide and the weather of the night before and conditions were perfect for hedgehog-harvesting. Unknown to others, Hobnail was blessed with three eyes: one 'seeing' eye, one blinded, 'greyed-out' eye for plotting and planning, and an unseen 'third' eye, hidden somewhere inside her head. It was only now and then that Hobnail had messages about what was going to happen. When her third, inner eye knew something, it was invariably important: sometimes, she realised she was in imminent danger; sometimes, she was told about a forthcoming storm so she could retreat to the Dark Hole rather than shiver in the wet and the wind which penetrated her tumbledown cottage with such ease; sometimes, she

53

understood what the Leaf Man was about to do — and then her greyed-out eye jerked into action to plot and plan and protect. This time, the inner message had been one of delight and she had gathered her Dear Ones quickly to race to the seashore to bag sea urchins for brunch.

The spiny creatures had suckered themselves onto rocks, their spikes standing to attention for protection and in the vain hope of trapping some decomposing delicacy which would ensure their survival until the water washed over them once more and they could return to their rocky seabed. Taking great care to avoid the stingers, Hobnail prised three prickly orbs from their resting places and popped them into a rusty bucket she had brought with her. Warty Toad's eyes bulged at the thought of the slippery, snotty insides which would soon be sliding down his throat. With a bit of luck, they could eat them here on the beach, without the unnecessary waste of time in travelling home. He watched Hobnail scoop salt water into the bucket to keep the creatures alive and fresh, and hoped she had remembered the stout knife which would be needed to pierce the sea hedgehogs' armour. Snidey Slug was not so excited. The urchins were not his favourite thing to eat. To him, they seemed a bit like distant sea cousins, on the inside at least. He settled himself in a kelp nest and sucked on a slimy sliver of the seaweed, enjoying the cool breeze which fanned his skin.

Seagulls mewed in disapproval, overhead. They had been whetting their beaks, ready to chop and slice through the spiky spheres themselves, so they swooped and shrieked, *"Mee-ine! Mee-ine! Mee-ine!"*

"I is thinking of boot-walking to my sea-cave, dearies," Hobnail told them, straightening her aching, hunched back as best she could after bending over her bucket. "I feels a beckoning and I wish to be rest-feeling in mind and body, if you please so."

The sea-cave was a place for her to rest and to think and to be quiet. It had only shallow lappings of water around its entrance right now and would be easy to reach, as the tide was at its furthest from the shore. The rocks, which made access treacherous, were no problem for Hobnail; she always wore her strong boots and she knew how to pick her way through the obstacles without tripping or slipping. The ice-cold plunge pools between, were to be avoided at all costs. No day-trippers ever tried to make their way to the cave; it was well-known that careless, curious people had drowned in the past. No beachcombers attempted it. There would be no children with nets and a foolish sense of adventure. Not even the wise fishermen would try. It was Hobnail's sea-cave and no one else's.

****

The shape of a large, black crow swooped in the sky above the beach. Crow-cus, the Baby-Snatcher, was spying. As ever, he kept his beady, bloodshot eyes fixed on his target and there was very little about Hobnail's movements, he missed. He would tell Liar-nel that she was wading out to the strange cave. What she would do there could only be guessed at, but at least they knew where she was, and they could wait. He circled a few times before the seagulls chased him away. He had no right to be there.

"Mee-out! Mee-out! Mee-out!"

"Crauk! Crauk!"

****

The imprints of her two sturdy boots stayed only briefly in the shifting sand near the entrance. Their mark was fleeting because the seawater was sucked into the tracks as soon as they were made, their shape blurring at the edges and then smoothing over as if they had never existed. Hobnail stood still to watch her footprints disappear. It made her feel safe. There was no trace for anyone to follow. It was as if she had never been there. She thought about the tunnels which were open at the back of the cave, rounded and twisting, made by the swooshing of ancient rivers and underground flumes. Although most were dry and navigable now, water still flowed through some of them, carrying the torrents of whirlpools and the gushings of waterways through rocks, to be spewed out further up the coastline, into the sea. Deep inside the sea-cave were bathing pools which Hobnail also knew well. She loved to indulge in an occasional revitalising, bracing dip — the only bath she ever had — the freezing temperatures making her skin glow and tingle, the cold making her feel alive! Stalactites hung down over these tarns, wet with cave water and mineral salts, as they grew, slow-drip by slow-drip. Their cousins, the

56

stalagmites, bulged from below, desperately trying to reach the roof of the cavern.

Hobnail had spent many hours exploring these passages and yet still did not know them all. She had taken a lantern with her, the first time. The lantern had a wick, soaked in lamp oil stolen from the town, and this she had lit without tinder, without a flint and without matches, but with the *magical electricity* in her extra fingers. The sixth finger on each hand had been seen as a disfigurement when she was born. It was one of the many reasons her mother did not love her and why others shunned her. As a child, Hobnail had felt the shame of being different. She tried to hide her hands whenever she was with anyone, tucking them up into the sleeves of her shabby clothing or holding them behind her hunched back. It had only been when she met her Great Aunt, Tabitha Wrinklewarts, that she realised these extra fingers were, in fact, a special gift.

"Six fingers?" Tabitha had queried, looking at the small child's hand in her own bear's paw. "Jolly useful. Extra-jolly useful, in fact. Lucky you!" and as they parted, she had told her, "I expect you to use your twelve fingers wisely; you will come to appreciate their powers in time."

And so she had. It really was *very* handy to be able to zap things when she needed to.

Spending time, exploring the passages underground, had led to the discovery of the connection to the Dark Hole. Like the others, this tunnel used to be a rushing cave river, but this one had streamed, with many twists and turns under the far, forest floor. Years after the water had ceased to flow down it, Hobnail had followed its trail from the opening in the cave, back through the rock, rising steadily upwards to her special hideaway under the long, green, slime fronds. It was a super-handy, secret link between the two. She had fashioned a tunnel door out of wood, on the inside of the Dark Hole, and she was confident no one would ever find it. She knew no one could get to the sea-cave and she knew no one would get past Great Boulder on the other side. She was sure of it. Usually.

Today, however, she was not so sure.

Something was different in her cave.

The *something* made the hairs on the back of her neck prickle and Hobnail felt a sudden flush of unease. As she stood there, watching the shifting sand at the entrance to her sea-cave, she noticed *other* footprints. They were about the same size as her own had been, but they were on the far side, a few steps away. They were deliberate, stealthy, slow footprints and they appeared, one after the other, as if someone was picking their way carefully between the rocks, heading from the sea, towards the opening of the cave.

But there was no *someone!*

The footprints appeared *all by themselves!*

As soon as one indentation was made, another step followed, and the first began to fill with seawater, blur at the edges and then smooth over, disappearing just as her own had. Then another step followed. And another. And another.

Hobnail was glued to the spot. It was as though the sand beneath her own feet had sucked so hard, she could not raise her boots. Her legs felt heavy and her heart began to pound. She screwed her fists up tightly, staring and staring at the footprints as they were made and then erased by the water.

How could this be happening?

Whose feet were these?

Was the person invisible?

"What strange tricksiness is appearing before me?" she murmured to herself in concern. "I is never seeings of such a thingummy before."

Her head turned ever so slowly as she watched the footprints reach the gaping mouth of her secret sea-cave and vanish inside. This made no sense. There was no boat moored nearby. There was no evidence of anyone, other than the mysterious footprints in the sand, and now, even these were gone. Perhaps, she had imagined them? Hobnail shook her head and ground her teeth, trying to work it out. Wake up inner eye! What was about to happen? It must have been a trick of the light; shadows of her own feet perhaps, or creatures underneath the sand making boot-like shapes, or old footprints re-emerging for some reason.

But none of these explanations reassured her.

Certain that she couldn't possibly leave without checking all was well, Hobnail dragged one boot against the sandy suction and took a step towards the sea-cave.

All was quite still.

There was nothing to be seen or heard.

She dragged her other boot out and took another step. So far, so good. Three more steps and she was standing inside the entrance, looking at the familiar form of the rocky walls. Nothing was out of place. There were the usual tunnel openings. There were the remains of the meal she had eaten last time, the empty mussels still discarded on the little rocky

59

seat where she had sat. For a moment, she cast a loving look at some seaweed threads with pretty shells, untouched, still swaying and dangling over a stone ledge, where a certain Baby Kipperling had been hidden for a while…

But then Hobnail noticed a smell.

It was only faint, largely masked by the lingering memory of stale fish, but it was definitely there. She wrinkled her nose and sniffed. Her sea-cave smelled undeniably rather odd. There was an underlying suggestion of something she recognised, but it was out of place here. She closed her working eye to allow her greyed-out one to think. When her eye was closed, her sense of smell became much keener. She took a slow, deep breath into her nostrils. Where had she smelled that before?

That was it!

Outside the old pub in the town!

Hobnail's eye jerked open. Of course! Tobacco from a pipe and just a hint, although still unmistakeable, of alcohol. Quite *which* alcohol it was, she had no idea. Hobnail had never been inside the pub as she would have been hounded out of the place immediately, but she had skulked past, in the shadows occasionally, and had smelled the smokers of pipes or cigarettes, and the drinkers of whisky and beer. Someone had been here. In her cave. And that someone was a smoker and they liked a certain sort of drink.

It was just as Hobnail was waiting for her greyed-out eye to come up with a plan that the footprints returned. This time, the sandy imprints were going in the opposite direction, out of the entrance of the sea-cave, and this time, they were deeper

60

and more hurried. One quickly followed the other and they appeared to be rushing out to sea, as if escaping before being caught. Hobnail's immediate reaction was to duck down behind a rock, to hide from who knew what or whom? Once more, her heart thudded in her hairy chest and she clenched her twelve fingered fists. More slowly this time, the footprints smoothed over, their depth taking a little longer to fill.

And then they were gone.

There was no trace of what Hobnail had seen, or thought she had seen.

The sea-cave felt less comforting right now. Usually, Hobnail felt secure and safe there, certain that she was alone and would not be disturbed in her humming or meditation. She had always felt welcomed, sheltered and soothed. Just now though, without any explanation of what had happened, she felt rather wobbly inside. A little bit sick. And a little bit cold.

Time then, to leave.

She looked out of the entrance of the cave and saw the sky had darkened since their arrival on the beach. A heavy cloud had built up and a slow drizzle had begun to fall. The spring sunlight no longer danced on the waves, glinting and flashing. Instead, the water had turned to a chilly grey which made her shiver. Casting a final glance behind her, into the depths of her cave, Hobnail began to pick her way through the rocks as quickly as she could. She was anxious to re-join her Dear Ones, to tell them of the mystery. Perhaps in the telling, some logical explanation would occur to her and all would be well. The three of them would talk together and consider all that had happened, and then in relief, they would laugh out loud and marvel at tricks of the light or shifting of the sands or how an imaginative mind can give you the heebie-jeebies. Perhaps her greyed-out eye, the eye of reason, plotting and planning, would come up with an answer at last. They would all enjoy their meal of sea hedgehogs and potatoes, feeling warm and happy again.

Feeling relieved and more reassured with these thoughts, Hobnail looked down at her feet, to check for slippery seaweed. Her boots, although robust, could skid easily just here and she didn't fancy falling into the sea — the drizzle had now become a steady rainfall and she was getting wet enough as it was. As she looked down though, to her surprise, she saw what she assumed was a piece of litter, dropped by a rock. Litter? Here? How? No one except her *ever* came here! She stooped to pick it up, her six fingers trembling slightly.

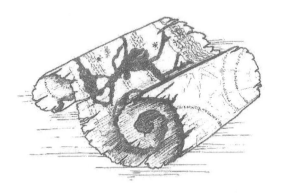

It was a scroll of paper.

The paper was old and brown and tatty.

The paper was a map of the sea-cave's tunnels.

****

Chapter Four
Map

As the spiny sea urchins smoked slowly over the fire, with potatoes wrapped in moss and softening in the hot embers, Hobnail was unusually quiet. Warty Toad and Snidey Slug were a little concerned. They had made their way back from the seashore with greater haste than usual — and without explanation. Bumping around in the bicycle basket, they had heard a few words escaping from their mistress's hairy lips, none of which had made any sense.

"Prints of feet I's seeing. Who-sies? Who?"

And —

"Coldness of belly in my sea-cave."

And then —

"Who is walking in my place of secrecy? Who?"

Try as they might, the Dear Ones had only caught snatches of her words as she panted her way home, cycling hard against the wind and rain. They had kept silent, looking at each other quizzically and not squabbling for once. Obviously, *something* was not at all right. Once home, the fire had been rekindled without fuss, the potatoes wrapped, and sea hedgehogs prepared. The two could tell Hobnail was troubled. It was only when the meal had been eaten, the sea urchins more

64

to Snidey's taste now they were cooked and rubbery rather than slimy, that she began her explanation. In the shadows cast by the dying fire, she gathered Warty and Snidey to her. They settled down together on the old, mouldy sofa whilst Lucy-fur listened to the conversation but stayed on the floor near one end, her eyes fixed on a dark corner, her ears alert and her ginger tail swishing.

"I is having something in my pocket of overcoat which gives me a worrisome tummy feeling, my dears," Hobnail began.

Warty Toad didn't understand how this could be the case. He knew his mistress kept all sorts of random things in her overcoat pockets, but she had always collected them herself, for special charms or recipes. She would bring home only those items she thought were of value to her. Why should she have something in her overcoat pocket that worried her?

"I is finding of something in my sea-cave and I has brought it home to consider." So saying, Hobnail reached into her pocket and brought out the piece of paper she had found by the rock. Warty Toad and Snidey Slug strained their eyes in the dim light to see it. Lucy-fur glanced up quickly but then, uninterested, resumed her watch.

The tatty scroll was curled up, and brown at the edges as if it had been rolled and re-rolled many times. The corners were folded and dog-eared; salt crystals and shiny grains of sand spilled from the creases. There were thumb and fingerprints all over it, smearing the writing, which made it indecipherable in parts. A hurried hand had penned it and the

65

writing appeared to have extra words added here and there, as after thoughts or when further detail had been needed. In places, the rough charcoal stick had broken through the paper, leaving words without letters and adding sooty smudges.

There was no doubt it was ancient.

"Has it come out of a bottle, do you think? You know like a letter in a bottle that some people throw into the sea?" offered Warty, by way of explanation. He knew that the paper could not just have been dropped at the sea-cave because nobody went there, except for Hobnail, and he realised that the very fact that it was there at all, was one of the things that bothered Hobnail the most. "Perhaps, a bottle floated in on the tide and smashed against the rocks, letting the paper out, from a desert island or somewhere, calling for help! Or maybe a child let it float on the water hoping it would reach a distant land. What does it say? Does it ask for a reply?"

"It's not a letter, stupid!" smirked Snidey Slug who could just about make out the line drawings and arrows, as well as the written notes. "It doesn't say, 'Dear Warty Toad, please rescue me!' Or, 'Dear Warty Toad, let me know how far my bottle went. Write back to this address…'"

Their mistress shushed them both through yellow teeth. Her greyed-out eye was doing its best to plot and plan but, without correct information or ideas, it was difficult to think what to do next. "That is being a sensible suggested notion, Warty, my pet," she murmured, in careful thought. "But is wrong being." Hobnail saw Warty look a little embarrassed. He was only trying to help. So, she continued, quickly, "You

66

is right that I has worries about how it got there, and I has no explaining of that just yet, but I is also mind-fears about the writing upon this paper." They all fell silent and thought hard. Certainly, there were two concerns.

Firstly, where did the paper come from? The 'letter in a smashed bottle' theory was good, except that it wasn't a letter. And there had been no smashed bottle. Nobody ever — *ever* — went to the sea-cave and so it couldn't be dropped litter. It could not be flotsam or jetsam, (Warty still struggled to remember the difference), because it was dry and so had not come in on the tide.

And, secondly, as Hobnail could see easily, the ancient scribblings on this worn, well-thumbed piece of paper showed that someone — *someone!* — knew the layout of the tunnels in her sea-cave. She had definitely not seen this paper before, so whilst it looked time-worn, thin and fragile, surely it must have been used recently and it must have *just* been dropped. *Someone*, at *some time* between her last visit and today's, had been there, to her private, secret cave.

And then Hobnail thought of the mysterious footprints.

The paper shook in her hands. She felt sick.

****

Fiblet and Fibkin, Liar-nel's special friends, dangled daintily from the Leaf Man's fingers as they lazed under the long, green, slime fronds. They swayed and swung backwards and

67

forwards in their leafy cocoons, wondering how to spend their time.

"I'm a bit fed up," commented Fiblet, twizzling idly on his twine. "Not getting many spy messages through, are we? I mean, Crow-cus has been in touch, but there wasn't that much to report: only told us that old Missus Twelve-Fingers was shuffling about the beach with a bucket, collecting weird, spikey things — and he was more concerned about being chased off by the seagulls!"

"Hmmm," Fibkin agreed, thoughtfully. "There isn't much going on at the moment. We haven't had a good bit of mischief-making for a while, now. We're just not getting any interesting information through, about her."

Liar-nel listened with amusement in the damp darkness underneath the long, green, slime fronds which dripped

and dropped,

and dribbled,

and drobbled,

and smiled his broad smile. "I have heard a little from the Mushrumps," he told them. "She has been to the Dark Hole with her two hangers-on, I believe."

"Hardly unusual, though," sighed Fiblet. "Her hair changed colour from grubby, grisly-grey to peculiar, putrid-purple, somehow, but that was all. The Mushrumps didn't even notice! It was the Moss-makers, busy with their knitting, who told us, *clack-clack-clack*!"

"Not that we're interested, of course," fibbed Fibkin.

"No! Of course not!" lied Fiblet. "She's of no interest to us at all."

"I mean, it's not as though it would be a good idea to take things into our own twiglet hands, is it?" queried Fibkin. "Just to check things out?"

"Are you suggesting that we do some spying, ourselves, my dear leaf-brother?" asked Fiblet, with a wink. "That would be a *dreadful* thing to do, my twig-twin. Apart from anything, we are so terribly busy, swinging and dangling." He swung and dangled for a moment, and then said, "Where do you suggest we go?"

"Well, I suppose we wouldn't find anything of any importance in the *Dark Hole*, for example, would we?"

"The Dark Hole? Hmmm…"

"I *mean*, there would be no purpose at all in having a secret peepety-peep?"

"Yep. You're right. None whatsoever."

At that, in one fluid, graceful movement, the Leaf-Man lowered his leaflettes gently to the mossy bank. He wet his smiling, smooth lips with a slip of his snake-like tongue, before resuming his camouflage and vanishing into the swamp tree bark.

****

Lucy-fur twitched suddenly. Her amber eyes grew abruptly bigger and black and focused. She gave a low growl and flattened her ears back against her head. She dropped her fluffy

69

tummy to the floor slates of the cottage once more and shuffled even closer to the old sofa which she had been guarding so carefully.

"Lucy-fur, my kitty-pet?" queried Hobnail, looking down at her from the scroll of paper she was studying. "Is you whisker-faced growling at a mousie?" The ginger cat did not turn her head at the question. Her tail began to lash, and her growl grew louder.

Warty Toad was alarmed. Things were not awfully tranquil this evening. First, there was the strange piece of paper which was so worrying for Hobnail, and second, the cat was still acting spooked. He tucked his head into his toady shoulders, as far as it would go, just leaving his bulging eyes wide open. Whatever was going on, he was going to hide, if necessary! He swallowed an uncomfortable lump in his throat with a gulp and tried to stay calm but, hearing another warning note from Lucy-fur, he decided it was *indeed* going to be necessary. He started to make a cautious move, one-toady-foot-after-the-other… and just reached his mistress's armpit, about to tuck himself into its dark safety… when Lucy-fur *leapt!* With claws splayed out from her front paws and a fearsome howl, she dived under the sofa as far as she could reach, smacking her pretty head so hard that a rip of the mouldy fabric fell away with the impact. Over and over again, she grappled and snatched with her tiger paws, frustrated that she couldn't quite reach her target. Growling and hissing, the feisty little cat tried and tried to attack, until Hobnail felt she

70

had to get to her feet to intervene, dropping Warty and Snidey to the floor as she did so.

"Goodness me of graciousness! Whatever's being under my sofa, kitty-cat?" she called out in surprise. "I wills be of turning it overs if that is of helpfulness to you!" And so saying, the grotty sofa was upturned with an unpleasant *whumph* of dust and a cloud of damp, cobwebby threads.

They all looked at the floor which had been underneath. It wasn't particularly clean, but there was nothing there.

Lucy-fur looked around her, wildly, searching for the missing prey. Where had it gone? Where *had* it gone? And why could she smell salty seawater and mouse about her whiskers, if there was nothing there? They all stayed quite still for a moment, wondering what all the kerfuffle had been about.

And then an unfamiliar voice from the cellar door rang out. "By my blade and my buckshot! By cuttle fish and cod! That were a shot across m' bow and no mistake, but I'm over here and not afraid. Only dogs show fear!"

Hobnail, Lucy-fur, Warty Toad and Snidey Slug were astonished. Exactly who was that?

****

The leaflettes were creeping through the dinge under the long, green, slime fronds. It amused them to be on a spying mission. They were bound to find something out. They were *determined* to find something out. Swinging and dangling

71

from Liar-nel's twiggy fingers was all very well, but they would rather be up to mischief and their favourite pastime was to make trouble for Hobnail. The Leaf-Man's other spies, Mr. and Mrs. Mushrump and the Moss-makers, found information occasionally but it always took a bit of time to come through. The Moss-makers had to knit and *clack-clack-clack,* or Mexican hand wave, to get their message across, and the Mushrumps were not the fastest movers on their fat, fungal feet, nor were they the cleverest of communicators. Crow-cus was keen and crafty without doubt, but his wings often got in the way. He was excellent at flying high over the cliffs and headland, searching the beach and shoreline, and he was skilled in his flights through the forest or above the chimney pot of the tumbledown cottage, but it wasn't always easy to navigate through the fronds when you had feathers. They could get wet, and tangled so easily. *Crauk! Crauk!* For the twiglets, Fibkin and Fiblet, however, it was easy-peasy to be sneaky. It was lemon-squeezy to be sly. Of all the spies Liar-nel had, they were the best. The plan was to make their way, on tippy tiptoes, through the undergrowth, to Great Boulder. Once there, they would attach themselves to a nearby swamp tree, like stick insects, and wait.

And wait.

And wait.

Until they found something out. Something of interest to Liar-nel. Something they could act on, to stop the old hunchback Missus Twelve-Fingers from coming into their domain. Something to frighten her away.

For good.

****

Hobnail felt decidedly on edge. She was sure there had been a voice but no one was there with her in her home, except for her Dear Ones. Was she hearing things as well as seeing things now? None of this made any sense. Mysterious footprints in the sand and now a mysterious voice. Nervously, she hobbled her way over to the cellar door and opened it, slowly. The familiar creak sounded the same. The dark mustiness was the same. There was the same damp sort of comforting smell of apple boxes and autumn stored nuts. There was no further noise or odd voice.

"Helloooo!" she called down the cellar steps. "Who is being in here, if you please so?"

There was no reply.

Tentatively, Hobnail placed one boot on the top step and peered into the dark. "I is saying, 'Helloooo'!" she insisted. "Is anyone's being in my cellar of storage?"

There was no reply.

There was no sound.

One cautious boot followed the other as she began to descend. There was nothing out of place. All seemed well as far as she could make out. Hobnail tried one last time. "Because, if there is someones being here, come out and be showing of yourself! I is not liking of this game, and you is wrong to be playing of it."

No reply.

No sound.

Hobnail shook her head and muttered a little. Then, trying very hard to be sensible, she climbed back up the steps and returned to the little, smoky sitting room, relieved to be back in the company of Warty, Snidey and Lucy-fur. She busied herself, putting a large pot of rainwater, collected from a hole in the roof, onto the fire to boil for a calming mug of lavender tea. As it heated up, she resumed her study of the paper scroll, determined to find some solution to the mystery of it all. Parts were clearer than others, but it was obvious that this was indeed a map of her sea-cave. She recognised most of tunnels and pathways on it, although not all. Whoever had drawn it had a better knowledge than she did and had made their way even further into the underground rocks than she had. She closed her good eye and forced her blind eye to think. What should she do? What would be a good plan?

It was just as the water began to boil for her cup of tea, Hobnail sensing the soothing steam rising in the air and breathing lavender in through her hairy nostrils, that a sound made her snap her eye open once more and catch a stifled scream in her throat.

"M'lady will come looking for it, y' know," called that voice.

****

Chapter Five
Visitor

At the sound of the voice, everyone in the little cottage was thrown into a panic. Hobnail sprang onto the upturned sofa, her boots landing with a great thud which made the springs twang, ping and break. Warty Toad leapt onto a pile of bricks and squeezed himself into a dark, dark space between them. Snidey Slug flattened himself down onto the floor slates so he resembled nothing more than something someone might have trodden in. Only Lucy-fur didn't want to escape. She scrabbled at the cellar door until it opened again and allowed her to pelt down the steps, disappearing into the darkness.

Eventually, her heart still pounding in her chest, Hobnail spoke. "It isn't just my ears a-tricksing me, then?" She peered cautiously at the cellar door, keeping a safe distance, still wobbling with shaky legs on the sofa. "Dids we all hear it?" She looked around to try to locate her Dear Ones, but all seemed to have vanished. "I is of wondering if it is my inner eye talkings and warnings me, but I thinks no! If we is all hearings the same voicey scariness, it must of real life in nature."

It was true. Hobnail had wondered for a split second whether her third eye was predicting the future for her, warning her of something that was about to happen, but if they had *all* reacted to the sound, it couldn't have been a voice in her head. And the voice *must* have been talking about the map. Whoever had dropped it must want it back and Hobnail didn't want whoever *it* was to pay a visit! She looked around her again, checking there was no immediate danger. What should she do?

The answer to that was simple. Run!

Run with the map and return it to the sea-cave, then whoever *it* was would get it back and leave them alone!

Without thinking twice about it, and certainly, without investigating the voice from the cellar, Hobnail stuffed the scroll of paper into an overcoat pocket and rushed outside. She jumped onto her bent bicycle and cycled furiously to the edge of the forest, bouncing off as she got there, leaving her wheels spinning in the wet grass. Never before had she dashed so quickly through the long, green, slime fronds! Never before had she been so careless in her movements! Never before had she felt so frightened! Great Boulder was woken with a sharp knock of stone and for once it rolled back without having a moment to grumble, allowing Hobnail to nosedive into the Dark Hole, where she plummeted to the dirty floor in a heap. The little wooden door at the base of the Forbidden Wall was thrown open and she hurried through her connecting, escape tunnel, keeping her head low to avoid bangs and bumps in her haste. Within minutes, Hobnail stood, panting and wheezing, in her sea-cave.

Although the cave was shadowy, she could see there was nothing out of place. There were no footprints to be seen. All was calm and only the sound of gentle, soothing lappings of the waves could be heard as they ran in hurried ripples onto the sand. Hobnail delved into her overcoat pocket and withdrew the tatty map which had caused her so much upset. Her hands were clammy, her hairy legs trembled and she felt rather queasy as she did so. Dropping it more or less in the same place as she had found it, she cast a quick look around her and then sped back to her tunnel, not at all wanting to be back at home to face *whatever* or *whoever* the voice belonged to, but worrying that her Dear Ones might need protection.

****

"Well I never, Mrs. Mushrump."

"Indeed, Mr. Mushrump."

"What do you think she's doing, Mrs. Mushrump?"

"Hard to say, Mr. Mushrump."

"She was in a bit of a hurry, wasn't she, Mrs. Mushrump?"

"That she was, Mr. Mushrump. That she was."

"Rushing about in a state, Mrs. Mushrump!"

"She was indeed, Mr. Mushrump. She was indeed."

"So why do think she was, Mrs. Mushrump?"

"Hard to say, Mr. Mushrump. Hard to say… but…"

"But what, Mrs. Mushrump?"

"Well, like I say, it's hard to say, but I think she was in a panic, Mr. Mushrump. In a panic, I would say."

****

Lucy-fur had given up the chase and, after an exhausting ten minutes of growling, hissing, sniffing and searching, she had made her way back to the room above the cellar. She was hugely irritated and could not stop the lashing of her tail. For days now, she had harboured serious suspicions about a rat and for days, she had been frustrated in her pursuit. In due course, feeling more settled, Warty Toad crept out of his hidey-hole and Snidey Slug unstuck himself oozily from the floor with a glutinous squelch. Together, whilst waiting for their mistress's return, they tried to work things out.

1. There had been a scroll of paper. It was obviously very old and had been dropped.

2. Hobnail had been very upset.

3. There had been a voice. It was obviously a strange voice and was a teensy bit threatening in what it said.

4. Hobnail had been startled by it.

5. *Most importantly*, what was there to eat?

There had been no food since the sea urchins and there was little prospect of getting any at the moment. Warty Toad decided that now, after all the excitement, he was feeling rather peckish. Not for the first time, he began to eye up Snidey Slug's soft, juicy body, but the thought of Hobnail's reaction if he ate her Dear One was too dreadful, so he dismissed the idea as soon as it crossed his mind. He needn't have fretted. When Hobnail entered the tumbledown cottage, relief all over her face to see her little friends safe and well, the first thing

79

she suggested was food. The old hens had obliged by laying a few more eggs and so, in no time at all, they were bubbling in a pot over the fire.

"All is well being, my dears," Hobnail told them as Warty, Snidey and even Lucy-fur gathered around her. "The mapsie is in the sea-cave returned and we is having eggsies for tea." She lifted the hot eggs from the pot and began to shell them onto chipped saucers. She pierced each yolk with a grimy fingernail, so they broke and ran in a gooey, delicious mess, ready to be slurped at by all. Their tongues licked eagerly at the saucers and Hobnail sucked her dripping, sticky fingers to make sure no drop was wasted. But then, someone spoke.

"Room for one more?" the voice asked. "My whiskers are a-twitching at the aroma, and I have to confess to being a tad partial to an egg or two. It's been a while since I had that last lot!"

Everyone looked up mid-slurp, immediately alarmed. For there, by the cellar door, was a rat. Strangely, he was a sort of *see-through* rat, but he stood up straight and tall, holding his thin tail in one scrawny paw.

****

Of course, it was not only the Mushrumps who knew of Hobnail's flight of fright under the long, green, slime fronds. Fiblet and Fibkin were on their reconnaissance operation and had heard Hobnail crashing towards them, even before they saw her. Straight away, their curiosity was aroused. Normally, the hunched, old crone would be quiet and careful. Normally,

80

she would be cautious and wary. Normally, she was quite tricky to track. This frantic rush through the long, green, slime fronds was most unusual and without doubt meant something serious was happening. The leaflettes had leapt out of Hobnail's path by springing onto a swamp tree root and, from their place of safety, they had seen how she had hastened towards Great Boulder. To their astonishment, she had made a return trip, just as speedily. Her great boot prints thundered past them, squelching through the moss in the opposite direction. What comings and goings! This investigation was suddenly *most* interesting!

****

Lucy-fur's ears flattened over her head. Her back was arched and puffed up with fur, as she stood high on her tiptoes. Her tail became a bottlebrush, her amber eyes dark and staring. A low, throaty grr-grr-grr-growwwwwwwl came from her, before she drew back her pretty, pink lips and hissed and spat, and spat and hissed. This rat was no ordinary rat. This rat smelled like a rat, sounded like a rat and postured like a rat, but… the vague outline of the cellar door could be seen right through him and Lucy-fur was confused and frightened.

"By my ears and whiskers!" exclaimed the rat, scratching an invisible flea. "I have never seen, in all my sea-faring days, a catty-puss so wild and scratchy! But little fluff-ball, I've come across many ratters in my time and I laugh in the face of danger. I embrace excitement! Come on and fight Romany Ratticus, the ruthless rodent, if you dare!"

Lucy-fur was dumbfounded. How very odd! Slowly, she slunk back to Hobnail's feet and crouched down low, swallowing the nervous drool as it collected in her mouth. This was one rat she wasn't going to take on.

Hobnail listened to her inner eye. All seemed quiet though. She was not receiving any agitated message of warning about this visitor. She closed her good eye so that she could plan her next move. Talk to him, she thought. Find out who he is and what he wants. Above all else, keep the Dear Ones safe! With a tense tone to her voice, she spoke. "I hears your words of bravery, rat. I assures you, my spitting, ginger darlie will stay here at my feet, but you must be of stepping out from the glooms of the door and present yourself to us, so we can gets to know you better."

Without more ado, Romany jumped forwards and stood before them, bowing low in an exaggerated fashion, sweeping one front paw on the floor, the other being tucked behind his back. "Allow me to introduce myself. My name is Romany Ratticus, ruthless rodent of the sea, defender of the *Jasmine Pearl* and shipmate to none other than the fearless Sea Robber, Marnie McPhee!"

Hobnail was intrigued. She was rather enjoying this rat's swagger, even if she didn't necessarily understand all of what he said. She smiled at him, baring her yellow teeth, and visibly relaxed. Warty Toad and Snidey Slug sensed the change in the atmosphere and began to breathe more easily. Lucy-fur watched suspiciously, determined to keep her distance.

"Why is you being so transparently see-through, Mr. Ratticus?" questioned Hobnail. "I is a-wondering if you is a ghostie or a ghoul, perhaps? I has seen some of them in my time and this is the only answer my mind is giving me."

"You are a perspicacious person of great perception, methinks!" Romany replied, twirling his tail. "You seem to understand what I am. Of course, I can be as see-through as I like, in the true nature of a ghost-rat." And so saying, he disappeared completely, whilst whistling a merry sea shanty tune, to let everyone know he was still actually there. After a few seconds, he reappeared, growing clearer and clearer until his form was as solid as any of theirs.

This was truly remarkable and Hobnail could not resist clapping her six-fingered hands together in delight. "That is being an excellent trick, Mr. Ratticus!" she exclaimed. "It has been taking me long hours and spell-practising to invisibilise *myself*! You is a very talented rat."

Romany regarded Hobnail with interest. "Twelve fingers?" queried Romany, never one to miss a detail. "You, m'lady, are a very unusual person. Methinks you have special talents too."

Hobnail almost blushed. This rat visitor was most charming! With sudden memory of her manners, she realised that they were all standing in front of Mr. Ratticus, egg dripping from fingers and sticky round their mouths, and she hadn't offered him anything to eat. Within minutes, she had organised some egg shell scrapings and a piece of stale cheese from down the side of the sofa. They all sat in companiable silence as he ate, Lucy-fur feeling a little calmer but staying wary, nonetheless. Once he had finished, the rat cleaned his

83

whiskers meticulously and began to explain where he had come from.

He told them he was in fact a pi-rat and had spent many happy hours at the helm of a ship until it had met with the great *Storm of Misfortune*, all pirates having been lost at sea, apart from one, Marnie McPhee. She had slashed valiantly at the fastenings of a little accompanying boat, the *Jasmine Pearl*, and he had leapt aboard to join her. After battling ferocious wind and waves, the two survivors had been washed up on a beach with wreckage all around them, as well as treasures from their sea robberies.

"So, you are a thief?" questioned Snidey, thoughtfully. "Is that a good thing?"

"There's been a lot worse than Romany Ratticus, the ruthless rodent, believe me!" the rat replied, an expression of amusement twitching at the corners of his mouth. "I have witnessed terrible things, the likes of which a slug can only *imagine*. That is the life of a pi-rat. Yes, I am a thief, but I steal only food — remember those eggs? The real pirates only take from those who have more wealth than they know what to do with. They have to make a living, y'know."

The Dear Ones and Hobnail listened with a mixture of admiration and horror as Romany told them how he and Marnie McPhee had rowed back and forth, to and from the sea-cave, so she could hide her treasures safely. He told them of the pirates' promise, of their loyalty and their honour. He told them how Marnie was determined to keep her 'pretties' hidden. Then, with great drama, he told them about their dreadful drowning and how she *still* would not leave her treasure until she worked out how to get it to her ghostly shipmates. A promise was a promise and should not be broken. He told them how Marnie had drawn her map, hiding it in the sea-cave so she could consult it whenever she returned. It had been on one of these visits to check her booty, that Romany had wandered off to explore. He had come across a tunnel at the back of the cave and, on scurrying through it, had discovered it led to a wooden door.

"My tunnel of escape and secretness!" Hobnail cried. "Is you finding my secret way through to my Dark Hole?" This was an unpleasant thought for her. She was certain that no-one, not even a rat, knew of her quick route between the sea-cave and the Dark Hole.

"Fear not, m'lady!" Romany reassured her. "I'm not one for tellin' tales. Your tunnel is quite safe."

Hobnail calmed down a little. He seemed to be a genuine sort of rat — and, after all, who would he tell? What would be the point? Romany continued to explain that, hidden in his invisible ghostliness, he had followed Hobnail one day as she made her way from Great Boulder to her little cottage and, from then on, had been making regular visits, largely to see if there was any food he could pilfer. They did all remember the disappointment of the eggs after the hair-dying. Now they knew who the culprit was, and Lucy-fur understood why she had been so certain she kept smelling rat!

Warty Toad was a little confused. He was also a little concerned that food rations would be smaller from now on. "Do you really have to eat, if you are a ghost-rat?" he asked. "Surely you don't need to?"

86

"Romany Ratticus, the ruthless rodent, has an appetite like no other rat!" declared Romany, with a certain amount of pride. "Whenever I take solid form, I need to gather my strength and I do rather enjoy a fresh egg or two." He hesitated for a moment. "But I have tarried here a while too long and must be elsewhere. I bid you all '*adieu*'." And so saying, he vanished.

****

Determined to find out exactly what was going on and report back to the Leaf Man, Fiblet and Fibkin poked around Great Boulder. They searched in vain for a crack to squeeze themselves through, but the huge door guard gave them no chink. No matter. They would get to the bottom of this mystery soon. Hobnail was bound to return to the Dark Hole before long. They only had to camouflage themselves carefully. And wait.

****

M' map! I 'ave to go back!

The *Jasmine Pearl's* ghostly silhouette was outlined dimly on the waves. It seemed to be floating aimlessly. Two shadowy figures were on board: one sitting, with oars in hand and pipe in mouth; the other, standing upright at the prow with a thin tail stretched out behind. The crescent moon played hide-and-seek in the dark, night clouds, casting shifting glimpses of the craft and its occupants.

"I dropped m' map, Romany," a sorrowful voice called. "I must find it. I must 'ave m' pretties. I can't leave 'em." The boat bobbed up and down in the water. "I've been keeping that map safe, Romany. I've been hiding it so well in that cave!" On and on the boat bobbed. "I must 'ave m' pretties, Romany!" the sing-song voice carried on, over the waves. "I can't leave 'em. A pirate's *promise* be a pirate's *promise* and should *never* be broken."

The shape of the pi-rat bobbed in rhythm with the boat.

"I can't leave, Romany. I can't leave this world wi'out 'em! I kept going back. I went back, like I said I would, wi' m' map, Romany." Smoke rings puffed from the pipe, rising and falling with the *Jasmine Pearl*. "But this time, I be disturbed, Romany! I be disturbed and in m' hurry, I dropped m' map! I dropped m' map, Romany!" Her voice rose to a cry. "I 'ave to go back, Romany. I 'ave to return for m' map and m'pretties! We can live in the sea-cave if I can't take 'em wi' me. We can live there. Me wi' m' rattie and always wi' m' pretties!"

As the boat was rowed on through the sea, the figure rested her oars and began to sing:

"I hid m' sweet pretties in yonder dark cave
'Cos, I promised m' maties their treasures I'd save.
The waves they did smite me and carried me down,
But I'm not going nowhere, e'en though I did drown.
It's been oh so long now — and m' pretties still stay,
And I'll sing m' sea shanty forever, they say."

The two eerie seafarers floated on in silence for a while, the waves carrying them.

After a few minutes, the pi-rat turned to face his shipmate. "M'lady, if I might be so bold," he began, whiskers trembling in the cool breeze. "When you have visited the sea-cave from time to time, I have been elsewhere — and have been there on a few occasions, in actual fact." The smoke puffs stopped and the blurry figure of Marnie McPhee leaned forwards, listening with sudden interest. The pi-rat continued. "When you visit, as you have done, from time to time, following your map to touch your pretties, wondering how to take them with you, m'lady, I go... *ratventuring*." The oars trailed in the water. The waves slip-slapped against the side of the boat. "I too go a-visiting, when you do, from time to time..."

The shadow of the Sea Robber shuffled impatiently in her seat. "What is it ye be telling me, Romany, eh? What 'as this to do with m' map? This time I dropped it and I can't find m' pretties wi'out it, and I can't leave wi'out m' pretties, so now I 'ave no hope of leaving. Ever."

"M'pretties are hidden in yonder dark cave
Cos, I promised m' maties their treasure I'd save,
But what do I do now? I'm out of my mind
Now I can't take 'em wi' me or leave 'em behind.
And it's oh so maddening, and here I 'ave to stay,
And I'll sing m' sea shanty forever, they say."

The silhouette of the pi-rat jumped down from the prow and faced that of Marnie McPhee. "Romany Ratticus, the ruthless rodent, knows no '*can'ts*'! Romany Ratticus, the ruthless rodent, knows no obstacles in life — or death! I have information to help in this situation of dire need, m'lady!"

The crescent moon came out from behind a cloud and shone over the *Jasmine Pearl*, the boat's shape shifting and changing; disappearing and reappearing. The furry shadow drew himself up in the breeze.

"Romany Ratticus, the ruthless rodent, knows who found your map, m'lady!"

****

Chapter Six
Wolfsbane

As far as Hobnail could make out, there was a problem which had to be dealt with. It was true that the riddle of the *Rat-whiff-and-vexatious-voice* had been solved, but it appeared they had a sort of come-and-go lodger. Charming and amusing as he was, Romany Ratticus, the ruthless rodent, had neither been invited to *stay* nor even to *visit*, which, Hobnail reflected, was a bit rude. Now, he had for the time being disappeared, but who knew when he would return? Worse than this, was another problem — indeed, a dilemma! The map had been returned to the sea-cave which was all well and good, but that didn't get rid of Marnie McPhee, whose ghostly presence when checking her pretties, quite frankly, gave Hobnail the willies. Her third eye had been sending her warning messages ever since Romany had explained the situation and Hobnail was certain that the Sea Robber was not going anywhere whilst her treasure remained.

"I is not wanting of any resident or thief in my sea-cave," Hobnail muttered to herself the next morning, after a troubled night's sleep. "And I is not wanting visitations of those who is not invited to my cottage. My door, although of swinging on its hinge in nature, is officially closed tightly shut so, to all uninvited rogues!"

Warty Toad and Snidey Slug listened sympathetically.

"Perhaps Marnie McPhee will get bored and leave?" suggested Warty, not really believing this to be the case, but trying very hard to be encouraging.

"I don't think so, Wart-Face!" snorted Snidey. "Romany told us she's not going anywhere until she can take her 'pretties' with her. Remember the pirates' promise? She's sort of stuck. She doesn't belong here, but she can't join her shipmates either."

"You is right thinking, Snidey, my pet," Hobnail sighed. The slug shot a smug look of satisfaction across to Warty Toad and then did a little 'told-you-so' wriggle-jiggle dance, his squishy body pulsating rhythmically.

Told-you-so. Told-you-so. Told-you-so.

"But," purred their mistress, reaching out to pet the toad, "Warty is *kind* thinking, which is thoughtful being of him and I is needing some hope."

Warty Toad's wide mouth turned up a little at the edges, as he turned to look at his snidey little friend. Ha!

"Anyways, my thinking and planning is this, dearies," Hobnail continued, using her greyed-out eye to consider her options. "I is going to checksy things out in my sea-cave. I plans to search for the pretty plunder by use of the mapsie. I has to checksy Romany's story is true because, although he is being a charmer and of amusing storytelling, you never can tells with rodents. They is crafty beings at the best of times."

92

She paused for a moment to think carefully. "Perhaps, also, I can be finding of this Sea Scoundrel," she murmured. "Perhaps, I can be telling of her to leaves us alone — if I am of brave enough heart!"

"Are you sure this is wise?" asked Warty, concerned.

"What if she's really fierce?" wobbled Snidey.

For a second, Hobnail felt a knot of anxiety form in her stomach. What if she *did* meet the pirate? An actual *ghost pirate?* And, she realised, a quiet ghost would be bad enough — but what if she really *was* fierce? She clenched her fists tight in sudden resolve. No one: pirate, ghost or rat, was going to stay in or continue to visit *her* sea-cave! She smiled at her pets. "I has a plan," she winked.

****

Fiblet and Fibkin were snoozing and swinging from a long, green, slime frond when Hobnail came treading cautiously through the moss and mud, later that day. She was wearing her old overcoat with the large pockets so, upon waking, the leaflettes knew she must be gathering again. Her twelve fingers were spread to each side of her and her good eye was darting quickly, surveying the undergrowth. The other eye was covered with its eye patch; a definite sign that she was cautiously planning her movements. The two spies became silently alert in an instant. How strange that she should have been crashing through the long, green, slime fronds yesterday, but was tiptoeing, today! As always, behind her, plopping through the wet, hopped the toad and bringing up the rear was the slug.

What was she searching for?

What was she up to?

Hobnail parted some leaves at the bottom of a swamp tree. They were frondy, feathery ferns which swayed prettily at her rough touch. They were not what she was looking for, though. Warty Toad plip-plopped to a standstill and blinked at the plant. Its plumy leaves fanned across his face for a moment, tickling his nostrils and making his nose peppery. He closed his poppy eyes and wrinkled up his warty face. He held his breath. He lowered his face into the moss. He tried really, really hard not to sneeze but… *warrumph*! He snorted and snotted into the wet greenery, taking in mouthfuls as he did so. They slithered down his throat in a sludgy, cold gloop.

"Shhhhh!" Hobnail shushed through yellow teeth. "Is quiet so, Warty! We is not wanting watchers and listeners to be seeing and hearing of us."

Warty Toad looked most apologetic and hung his head. He hadn't meant to sneeze, and he certainly hadn't meant to swallow a great gobbet of sloppy slush. He knew how important it was for silence. They should always be aware of the Leaf Man and his minions. Immediately, the moss at their feet rippled as a message was sent. The Moss-makers knew they were there.

Clack! Clack! Clack!

"Perhaps," whispered Snidey Slug. "If you told us what you're looking for, we could help. Our ears and eyes are much

94

nearer the ground you know, Mistress." As ever, he was keen to be the first to find something for Hobnail. He always wanted to be extra special.

"Snidey, I is looking for wolfsbane," he was told. "It is being tricksy to find and — be warned — it is deadly in the handling!"

The Dear Ones were alarmed. If Hobnail said something was poisonous, she was not joking. She had learned all about plants and poisons from her Great Aunt, Tabitha Wrinklewarts, when as a girl, she had visited and been told over and over: 'Know your poisons! Know your poisons!' The lessons she had learnt that day had never been forgotten and Hobnail treated all foliage with the utmost respect. Of all the toxic plants, wolfsbane was known as the 'queen of poisons' and needed to be treated with extreme caution. Its spikelets of purple flowers could be spotted easily, hanging on tall stems with dark green leaves, ready to brush against an unsuspecting passer-by, causing immediate numbness, and prickles, and pins and needles. Hobnail had been taught *never* to lick her fingers in a garden; if the slightest part of wolfsbane root was swallowed, she knew her problem wouldn't just be pins and needles...

Wolfsbane could cause a sudden and painful death.

Warty Toad and Snidey Slug were not at all keen to find it now. Gone were all thoughts of helping. Gone were all thoughts of being favourite or special or the first. They kept their distance from Hobnail as she searched. Let the expert deal with this one!

Fiblet and Fibkin heard the conversation and watched the gatherers with interest. Why should the old crone need a plant like wolfsbane? Perhaps, they both thought with a snigger, she would gather some and poison herself by mistake! That would get her out of the way, once and for all. That would leave the place under the long, green, slime fronds peacefully dripping

and dropping,

and dribbling,

and drobbling,

without her getting in the way. The Leaf Man would have his realm all to himself, at last!

As Snidey slithered and Warty plopped along behind Hobnail, they were troubled by the same question. What was her plan? Why did she need something as scary as wolfsbane? Where would they find it?

They would have their answers soon.

Both watched as their mistress parted some stems very slowly, using a swamp tree twiglet. Carefully, carefully, the purple flowers were gathered, using clumps of moss to protect her wizened hands and the dreaded wolfsbane was pocketed, lickety split.

****

Safely together in the Dark Hole, underneath Great Boulder, an evening fire smoking gently, the three shared some woodlouse jam, sandwiched between sorrel leaves. Warty knew it was time to eat and he would certainly *never* refuse the opportunity, but his stomach felt a little bit odd. It sort of gurgled a bit too much. He wasn't really, truthfully hungry, but he didn't want to let his share of the delicious meal go to Snidey. He remembered the mouthful of green slop he had swallowed and belched rather loudly. A little bit of icky, green sludge came up into his throat. It tasted horrid. Quickly, he swallowed it down, but he still felt a bit peculiar. Hobnail did not notice his discomfort, finishing her food with a satisfied smile.

"I is telling you now of my plans that are afoot," she announced.

"Erm, Mistress," queried Snidey, puzzled. "How can 'plans' be a 'foot'?" He looked at Hobnail's boots but could see no plans upon them.

Hobnail sighed, ignoring the question, and went on to explain. "I is having an idea from Romany Ratticus, the ruthless rodent. He is a clever disappearing rat, being of ghost in nature, and that has got my plotting eye thinking and planning. Is you wanting to hear what I has been reminded of?" The two Dear Ones recognised the signs of a story and, without hesitation, took up their positions, one on her shoulder, the other nestled under an armpit. Hobnail began to explain.

****

Although, as a child, she had learnt much from her Great Aunt, Tabitha Wrinklewarts, Hobnail had also attended special meetings as she grew up. These meetings occurred infrequently, and only when the moon was in the right phase, or the season, or the weather, or the tides of the sea were aligned in a certain way. She was never invited to the gatherings, as such. She had never received an invitation or letter in her sad, lonely life, but there was an unmistakeable tingle in the sixth finger of each hand when the time was right. It was as though a message was conveyed to her through the mists of the night or the dew of the morning, and the tingling was not to be ignored. She never had to wonder where or when the meeting would be; her third, inner eye gave her all the information she needed, and Hobnail knew all she had to do was to follow instructions and turn up.

Years ago, one chilly night when the moon was full and round and bathed in pale blue, the tingle in Hobnail's fingers had become insistent and she knew an important meeting was at hand. Within the hour she had arrived, shivering with cold and excitement, nervously looking around the clearing in the woods. A big bell started to clang. *Clang! Clang! Clang!*

Dark figures, like her, appeared from behind trees and from beneath bushes. They crept or sneaked or strode into the clearing. Some were tall, some were short; some were wrapped up so much you could barely see their features, whilst others jutted out their poky chins and hooked noses from underneath wrappings, peering at each other suspiciously. None of them spoke. Everyone simply inclined their head in acknowledgement and began to hum, as the wind moaned low through the shadowy trees. One by one, they took up position in a circle around one huge slab of stone, on top of which stood a wise, old woman, swinging the great bell in her hairy hands, her knuckles white in the moonlight.

The clanging was enough to waken the dead.

"Welcome to one and all!" she called once the bell had tolled for the last time. "Welcome to the young and to the old! Welcome to the tall and to the short! Welcome to the virtuous, to the wicked, to the beautiful and to the foul. Welcome to the ghosties and the ghouls, for we are aware you are amongst us." She paused to smile, knowingly. "Welcome to the newcomers and those who we know have entered our circle before!" She produced a tatty sheet of paper and stubby pencil, and proceeded to call out names, ticking them off theatrically. There was:

✓ Joanie Brimblebottom

✓ Alice Spite-Tongue

✓ Bearded Henrietta.

Then came:

✓ Delilah Deaf-Ears

✓ William Dog-Breath

and, of course,

✓ Tabitha Wrinklewarts.

At the other side of the circle were:

✓ Jon-the-Joker

✓ Michael Malice

✓ Weeping Wilhelmina.

A grey, ghoulish mist wrapped itself around the feet of:

✓ Barbarous Barbara

✓ The Silent One

and, of course,

✓ Hobnail.

Satisfied that all were present, the old woman tucked her tatty list into her hairy bosom to keep it safe for next time and so the meeting began.

Jon-the-Joker was presenting item number one. Apparently, he had discovered a new way to increase personal powers. Hobnail was not particularly interested. She had all the power she needed in her extra fingers, and, in any case, no one could ever trust a single thing Jon-the-Joker had to say.

Item number two was from Weeping Wilhemina. She sniffled and sobbed her way to the centre of the circle and, blowing her hooked nose into an enormous, soggy handkerchief, she explained how to polish copper basins so that the future could be seen within them. "Although, the dreadful trouble with this," she wept, "is that sometimes I don't want to know what *is* going to happen, because it spoils the *fun*!" She wrung the handkerchief out, tears pouring down her face. "And then, sometimes, the future is too *awful* to contemplate!" She paused to boo-hoo loudly. The others shuffled a little awkwardly and waited for her to calm down. "I sometimes wonder why I try to be a fortune teller at all!" she bawled. "The responsibility can be *unbearable*!"

The old woman who had called the meeting intervened, telling Wilhemina that this wasn't a therapy session and she should return to her place in the circle. Hobnail grew a little impatient. She could see into the future herself, by means of her inner, third eye. She didn't need to bother with all that copper basin polishing nonsense.

After a new cure for whooping cough, offered by Tabitha, consisting of trapping a long-haired caterpillar in a bag and

101

tying it around the ill person's neck, and then a short-cut method for wart removal, the meeting was almost at an end. The wise, old woman clapped her hands together to silence the murmuring that had started as all began to discuss what they had learnt. "My dear friends, I assume all problems and issues have been dealt with?" she enquired. There was a vigorous nodding of heads. "Then allow me to give you all a small present, courtesy of Bearded Henrietta." She produced a velvet bag which had been left, shyly, on the stone slab by the bearded one. The bag was passed around the circle and each member of the meeting took out a small, neatly folded bundle. Hobnail received hers and bobbed down to offer thanks. She unwrapped the gift carefully and found, to her great delight, that there, dangling in front of her eager eyes, was a magical snakeskin. She watched it sway in her fingers for a moment, entranced by the shimmering scales and then tucked it up a knicker leg for safe-keeping. She knew exactly what to use that for!

After a quick chat and mingling over moon-drop tea and fire-stick toffee, it was time to leave. The evening had been interesting. It had been good to have some company. It had been good to catch up with Great Aunt Tabitha, albeit briefly. It had been *very* good to receive a present — Hobnail had received very few in her miserable life — and so, before long, she was back in her tumbledown cottage, having hung her precious snakeskin on a shelf on the Forbidden Wall in the Dark Hole. As she slept that night, Tabitha's words from years before, danced in her head: *"Wrap seeds of wolfsbane in lizard skin and carry it with you to become invisible at will. Frightfully good fun! You must try it."*

****

Snidey Slug had listened to all this with great interest, but he felt sure that Hobnail had made a mistake. He wriggled from her shoulder to whisper in her ear. "Mistress, I think there is something wrong with this story."

Hobnail raised an eyebrow and narrowed her eyes. "Is there being, Snidey, my pet?"

"You have collected wolfsbane."

"That is right so."

"But you have a *snakeskin*."

"Is right so."

Snidey hesitated. He wasn't at all sure he should correct Hobnail because after all, she was the one who knew what Great Aunt Tabitha had said, but he *did so* want to appear clever. He took a breath and drew himself up, all prim and knowledgeable. "If you are going to use it for invisibility, Mistress, you need *lizard* skin, not snake!"

There was an ominous silence…

A few worrying seconds passed.

Snidey swallowed a sort of nervous swallow.

And then Warty was sick. He had dragged himself out from under Hobnail's armpit, just in time. Snidey Slug watched with disgust. Still Hobnail was silent.

"Mistress?"

"Snidey?"

"Warty Toad's just been slimy sick. Yuck!"

Hobnail smiled. "Clear it up then, Snidey," she instructed. "There's a good slug."

****

Chapter Seven
Invisibility

The leaflettes were in.

The next morning, Great Boulder had opened up a chink to allow Snidey Slug to slither sulkily through to the wet moss, so that he could wash off Warty's sick. Fiblet and Fibkin, ever alert even when swinging and dangling, saw their chance and slipped down the long, green, slime frond as fast as firefighters down a pole. Without a second's hesitation, they had scrambled to the crack which exposed the Dark Hole and, holding their arms and legs tightly against their stick bodies, had catapulted themselves over the edge. Just a couple of twigs blown in. Easy as that. Now the Leaf Man's spies could really find out what Hobnail was up to!

****

The snakeskin, taken from the Forbidden Wall, swayed in Hobnail's hand, her six fingers entwined through the delicate casing. It was quite thin and long — too long for the number of wolfsbane seeds which were cosseted inside the wilting, purple flowers which she had carefully laid out on a rock. Not a problem. She was sure she could tie a knot in the skin and make a little pouch. Warty Toad and Snidey Slug watched from a cautious distance as their mistress prised open the petals of one blossom and scratched the seeds out, using her long fingernails. She was extremely careful not to touch any part with her skin. Once all the seeds had been collected, they were gathered together in a little pile and Hobnail washed her fingertips in a chipped mug of rainwater. "Is perfect," she declared. "Now, for my skin of serpent!"

There was a slight noise from a corner of the Dark Hole.

A sort of skittering.

The spell-maker turned to look for a brief moment but all she could see were a couple of twigs that the wind had blown in. She turned back to her snakeskin and, using a pair of tweezers, proceeded to drop the seeds of wolfsbane into it, holding it up high so they would reach the tail end. "Wrap seeds of wolfsbane in lizard skin and carry it with you to become invisible at will," she muttered. "Lizards, snakes, snakes, lizards. All is being the same skin sort. Pie-easy, I is thinking, my dears!"

When the last seed was deposited, making sure that none had fallen on the floor or were still stuck to the tips of her tweezers, Hobnail slid two fingers down either side of the skin to make it flat and tied a knot deftly, a few centimetres from the tail. "Is you knowing where my snippety-shiddies are?" she asked her pets.

Snidey, eager to make amends after his impertinence of before, was already on it. He nudged a pair of rusty scissors towards his mistress and waggled his eye-stalks at her.

"Thank you, my precious," Hobnail nodded, picking them up. "Is helpful being of you."

The slug breathed a sigh of happiness. Oh, the relief of being in favour once more! The snakeskin was cut above the knot, like the cord of a baby, and the rest of the skin fell to the ground. The pouch was complete.

Hobnail promptly vanished from sight.

****

"She picked some flowers, didn't she, Mrs. Mushrump?"

"That she did, Mr. Mushrump. That she did."

"What did she want them for, Mrs. Mushrump?"

"That's hard to say, Mr. Mushrump. That's hard to say."

"But you're a lady, Mrs. Mushrump, you're a lady!"

"I know I'm a lady, Mr. Mushrump!"

"Well?"

"Well, what?"

"What will she do with the flowers, do you think, Mrs. Mushrump? What will she do with them?"

"It's hard to say, Mr. Mushrump, hard to say."

"But why is it 'hard to say' Mrs. Mushrump? You're a lady, Mrs. Mushrump. Why is it 'hard to say'?"

"I've never been given any flowers, Mr. Mushrump."

****

Fiblet and Fibkin had not seen this coming. They could not understand where Hobnail had gone. Although they had seen her snakeskin seeding and snipping, they thought her mutterings had been nonsense; just the ramblings of a demented mind. One minute she was there, busy tying and clipping, and the next, she had disappeared. They were not to know that within seconds of her disappearance, she was making her way, invisibly, through the secret passage to her sea-cave, leaving her Dear Ones behind for safety. They were not to know that she had a plan to check the map, find the pretties and look for a ghostly Sea-Robber. All they knew was that they were in the Dark Hole with Warty Toad and Snidey Slug.

Just them. Together.

And the fun of it all was — the *best* bit was — the stupid toad and the silly slug had *no* idea.

****

The cool air of the sea was a comfort to Hobnail. She took great breaths in through her hairy nostrils and relaxed a little. This felt safer. Being invisible meant she could investigate without being found. All she had to do was to pick up the map and follow the information on it. If what the rat had said was true, there would be hidden treasures which she had not found on her own exploration of these tunnels. If she *did* find them, she would have a real explanation for the mysterious footprints and the tatty scroll of paper. She would have the proof she needed to believe the rat's story. Then she would have to consider how to deal with a certain Marnie McPhee who was taking liberties with her sea-cave and needed to be told to leave!

To her relief, there were no appearing and disappearing footprints today, apart from her own, but there, over by the rocks where she had dropped it in her panic, was the map that Hobnail needed. She stooped to pick it up in her grimy hands. Turning it this way and that, she worked out how to follow the marks and scratchings. Had Romany really been telling the truth, then? Were there really pirate pretties hidden in these depths? Hobnail crept to the back of her sea-cave where the tunnels began to wind their way into rock. Excited now, she rubbed the sixth finger on each hand, encouraging the magical electricity to flow so that they glowed gently and gave her just enough light to see by. To one side of her usual route, was a small opening that she had not noticed before. It was concealed in the shadows, making it easily overlooked. Hobnail squeezed through, briefly squashing sea-ferns which were growing valiantly in a tiny crack where the thinnest of light beams seeped in from outside. The ground beneath her feet was sandy at first, and then became gritty, making a slight scrunching noise as her unseen boots trod with care. Her wizened, invisible hands felt along the rock walls, little fingers lighting up sacred, ancient paintings, their lines simply drawn. The brush strokes told tales of saintly heroes and slain dragons. There were carvings of grinning gargoyle faces amongst twisting fossils of serpentine worms. Despite the unease she felt amongst these cave creatures, Hobnail could not help a thrill of exhilaration. Here was a new passageway through her underground world! Here was evidence of times gone by. Here was real history beneath her fingertips! Time and again, she consulted the scroll, looking around her to locate signs and match them to symbols drawn by an unknown hand.

And so, the fizzing spheres of light made their way further and further into the rock.

****

Two twiggy sticks raised themselves from the floor of the Dark Hole. Each sprouted arms and legs as they sprang to their feet right in front of Warty Toad and Snidey Slug.

Snap! Crack! Click! Clunk!

"Ta-dah!" Fiblet and Fibkin rested their spiky hands on their hips. "Well, hello, Warty-Wart-Wart."

Warty shuddered and gulped. He felt sick all over again.

"And how are you, Snidey-Slop-Slop?"

Snidey forgot how to breathe, all of a sudden.

The two leaflettes looked at each other and tutted.

"Not very welcoming, are they?" Fiblet remarked.

"Bit rude, I'd say," replied Fibkin.

Both Warty Toad and Snidey Slug knew this meant trouble. They had met these two, spiteful sticks before and had never wanted to see them again. They also knew they were without their mistress and would have to be very careful indeed. Warily, Warty took a slow step towards the slug. Sensibly, Snidey slunk towards the toad. Safety in numbers. Each pressed their soft body tightly against the other, squishing together. They felt a little bit bigger that way, somehow.

"What togetherness! How very sweet!" smirked Fiblet.

"Very," sneered his brother. "You could say it was 'touching'." And the twig-twins chortled in delight at their fun.

The two Dear Ones kept glued to each other. They had no idea what to say or do and so they kept very quiet and very still.

"The toad looks very like a stone, don't you think, Fibkin?"

"Now you come to mention it, he does," came the amused reply. "And the slug looks like a poop."

Snidey coloured in embarrassment. This was awful!

"I think," continued Fiblet. "We should take a look around to see if there's a dustpan and brush to clean up a bit, don't you?"

"That's an excellent idea, brother. After all, we can't have dirty stones and poops littering the floor, can we?"

The Dear Ones opened their eyes wide in alarm. This was terrible!

Thoroughly entertained, the leaflettes began to explore the Dark Hole, Hobnail's special hideaway place, pretending to look for a cleaning brush. Helpless, Warty and Snidey watched as their unwelcome visitors poked and prodded and pried. The two baddies jumped and pinged about on the seagull feather sack which was Hobnail's makeshift bed. They swung from the cobwebs which festooned every corner, disturbing spiders which scurried into tiny cracks in the rock walls. (Warty Toad tried to remember which cracks they had run into, in case he needed some supper later, but then the thought made him feel even sicker, so he decided to forget them.) Fiblet and

112

Fibkin found jars and bottles and boxes, with lotions and potions and powders. They found Hobnail's tonics and slimes and poisons. Each one was knocked and rattled and shaken. The glow worms in their glass bottles were woken up, their light creating sinister shadows of the intruders onto the walls of the Dark Hole, making them look tall and even more menacing.

"Can't find a dustpan *or* a brush, Fibkin," winked Fiblet.

"Nope, neither can I," Fibkin winked back. "But I am rather enjoying looking through all these interesting things to be played with. What fun!"

And then, Fiblet and Fibkin found the Forbidden Wall.

The Forbidden Wall was exactly that. Forbidden. Warty Toad and Snidey Slug could go near it only with special permission and only with very good reason. Other glow worm lamps were shaken, lighting up the Wall's containers of red and black beetles, wood lice, worms, dung flies and bird bits. To the Dear Ones' horror, these were knocked to the dusty floor of the Dark Hole where the lids fell off, scattering the contents in the dirt. All Hobnail's collections of pecky, poky beaks, claws and birdsongs were released, the notes sounding shrill and startled as they escaped, echoing and bouncing off the walls. The jar which held rotting swamp tree bark was emptied, filling the air with a stomach-turning stench, and the charm stick sheep bones were thrown down with a clatter.

Warty Toad found his voice at last.

"STOP!" he shrieked in desperation. "STOP WRECKING EVERYTHING!" His popping eyes were bulging in dismay as fearful Snidey shook and quivered next to him. "WHY ARE YOU DOING THIS?"

The twig-twins stopped their game of destruction to consider this outburst. Fiblet looked at Fibkin. Fibkin looked at Fiblet. They shrugged their stick shoulders.

"Is that stone shouting, Fibkin?"

"I do believe so. I can't imagine what the matter is."

"You must STOP!" squawked Warty in panic. "*We'll* get the blame for all this mess because *you* are just two leafy sticks and then *we'll* be in terrible trouble and she'll squib us with her tortoiseshell spike and —"

"Deary, deary me," commented one fibber to the other. "That would be really, really dreadful! Don't you think?"

"Frightful. Appalling. We'd hate that to happen!"

Warty was about to add something else when Snidey Slug shushed him through thin, pursed lips, not wanting to make things worse than they already were. This was a shocking situation. What on earth were they going to do?

****

Despite the light from her glowing fingers, the map was becoming increasingly difficult for Hobnail to follow. The creases of the well-worn folds blurred some of the writing and she was at risk of taking the wrong turning. However, the air in this deep tunnel held an odour. Hobnail closed her good eye

115

to heighten her sense of smell. It was the unmistakeable pong of pipe tobacco and an accompanying whiff of grog! These smells were becoming rather familiar. Undeniably, she was on the right track. As she pressed on further into the cave, Hobnail's nose led her, twisting and turning, up and over, under and through, until one of her boots kicked against something hard. She opened her eye in surprise and there, at her feet, was a wooden crate. Behind it were a couple more. At the right of her, under a shelf of overhanging rock, was a fourth. The lids and hinges looked battered and rusty, and not all were fastened securely. A quick peep inside told Hobnail all she needed to know.

Romany Ratticus, the ruthless rodent, had been telling the truth!

The pirate pretties *did* exist. A few gold doubloons fell through her six-fingered hands as she scrabbled inside a crate. There were gold chains, crucifixes and pendants. There were brooches, bracelets and buckles. Hobnail's heart thumped in her hairy chest. This was exciting! This was amazing!

And this was a tinsy bit scary.

These treasures did not belong to her and she should leave them exactly where she had found them. Hobnail knew the difference between right and wrong. But who would know they were there though, except for her? Romany, of course, but he was only a rat — and a ghost one at that! Hobnail paused in her crate rummaging. Without doubt, some of these were not just pretty. They were *beautiful* and she had very little beauty in her life. She listened carefully for the sound of

116

footsteps, or the voice of a stranger, or heavy breathing from the darkest of the corners, but she heard nothing. Hobnail was sure she had not been followed. After all, who would have *seen* her? She considered the crates' belongings once more. They were like flotsam and jetsam, really. They must have been thrown overboard or floated away from the wreck of a ship at some time, surely? She tried very hard to dismiss the thought of pirates attacking and stealing. That had been in the past and this was the present.

It was all very tempting.

Hobnail's inner eye woke up. It told her to be cautious. It told her to be alert. It told her to be aware of a future meeting.

Her greyed-out eye told her to think carefully. It reasoned and planned with her, thinking through her options with care. It would be bad to take things that did not belong to her. But just a *couple* of items? Certainly, it would be foolish to take too many but, just *two*? That would be enough to please her without getting into too much trouble. Wouldn't it? Her inner eye became silent. Hobnail made her hands into fists, so her old, swollen knuckles cracked. She couldn't stay much longer. The invisibility charm was all well and good, but she ought to be getting back. Grabbing a wine goblet which had taken her eye, and a particularly fine jewelled ring which she forced onto a knobbly finger, she turned and retraced her steps out of the tunnels. She decided she did not feel guilty. She had squared it with her conscience. This was just rent for the storage use of her sea-cave. Fair and square.

****

"What a pretty dish!"

"It does look rather special, Fibkin."

"I think it's made of shell."

"Extra special, then. And fragile."

"And it's balanced so precariously on this shelf. Wouldn't it be frightful if it fell, with a great, big crash?"

"Tragic."

"Whooops."

****

Chapter Eight
Spies

In a rush of eagerness, Hobnail burst through the secret, wooden door at the bottom of the Forbidden Wall, clutching her newly acquired goblet in a beringed hand. Dropping the snakeskin pouch to the floor and becoming visible once more, she cried: "Is true, my Dear Ones! I *is* finding pirate pretties in my sea-cave! Looks you at this!" She held the prized goblet aloft. "And this!" She tugged at the jewel on her knobbly finger. "Romany Ratticus, the ruthless rodent, is a Rat of Reliability," she declared, oblivious to the chaos around her. "He is telling of us abouts Marnie McPhee and her pretty treasures and her findings of my sea-cave, her mapsie and drowning-glug-glugs — and is *true* so! Caskets and chests of gold loveliness in tunnels are lying. My own cave is being full of beauty jewellations!" She grinned breathlessly, all yellow teeth and excitement. "Great Boulder!" she called to the fat rock above her head. "Opens up for us so we cans hurry quick fast home for a meal and a thinks of what to be next doing." Great Boulder groaned and ground itself into a new position, letting some light and fresh, damp air into the Dark Hole. Suddenly realising she was getting no response from her Dear Ones, Hobnail stopped. "Warty? Snidey?"

She looked around in the pale light. Then she noticed the empty red and black beetle containers, their lids off in the dirt. She saw the pecky, poky beaks and claws from her bird bits' collection. She sniffed the smell of escaped rotting swamp tree bark and found its unfilled jar, toppled from its shelf, on one side. She spotted the sheep shoulder and rib bones, scattered amongst broken bits of... broken bits of... broken bits of...?

Her screech shattered the empty bottles, glass catapulting around the Dark Hole.

"WHAT'S HAS BEEN OF HAPPENING HERE?"

Deafened, Warty Toad and Snidey Slug were once more huddled together for protection. Warty wished he were indeed a stone, and Snidey hoped fervently that he really did look like a poop. Both shook uncontrollably. Neither dared speak to explain the events and defend themselves. Neither dared breathe. They were mortified.

There was a tiny titter of laughter, and a small skittering sound broke the silence for a few seconds. Hobnail swung round in her boots, but nothing was to be seen. She breathed heavily through her hairy nostrils. "WARTY TOAD! WHERE ARE YOU?" she yelled. "This is lookings like one of your clumsinesses! Be presenting of yourself to me, directly!"

Warty Toad knew he had no choice. He knew that on occasion, he had been a rather clumsy buffoon. On occasion, he *had* spilt or broken or dropped things. On occasion, he *had* tripped over, or slipped in, or crashed on top of things. He also knew that he couldn't pretend to be a stone indefinitely and he had to breathe sooner or later. Taking in a sudden, big gulp of

120

air, he puffed up from his position on the floor of the Dark Hole and blinked his poppy eyes in the direction of his mistress. Hobnail espied him immediately and narrowed her good eye to glower at him. Without saying a word, she removed her tortoiseshell spike from her hair where it was kept and flicked the end with one finger. The tapered barb quivered backwards and forwards. Warty Toad swallowed although he seemed to have no spit; his bulging eyes were transfixed on the pointed quill. He almost fainted at the thought of what was about to happen. He *dreaded* being squibbed! This tortoiseshell spike had been used before, on Great Boulder's bottom, and he remembered too well how he had closed his eyes and winced. Both he and Snidey had always known that this was the worst punishment and both had feared the day when it might be used on them.

Hobnail bent down low so he could feel her icy breath on him. "You hads better be thinking of good answerings, Warty," she whispered, threateningly. "I is only small seconds away from pinnings you to the wall by your feets and leavings you to hang there! *WHAT* has you done to my shell dish of beauty?"

Snidey Slug heard all of this. He knew Hobnail was wrong. He knew Warty Toad would be so terrified his voice wouldn't work. He knew what had happened and that he should speak out. It was a brave thing to do, though. He didn't like to put Hobnail right on *any* matter after the business of the snake-lizard skin confusion. What if she didn't listen to him properly, flying into a rage and pinning him to the wall, too?

The slug heard his matey stuttering and stammering, attempting to make noises but no words were coming out of his dry, warty lips.

"I is beginning to counts, Warty Toad. Onesies... Twosies... Threesies..."

"STOP!" squeaked the poop on the floor. "It *wasn't* him!"

Hobnail looked astonished at the boldness of her other pet. He was usually so quiet and weedy. Then she flashed a glare of fury at him and took a stride forward. "Is you tellings me I is wrong, Snidey Slug? *AGAIN?* Is you tellings me I am spikerating the *wrong* culprit in this?"

"Yes," mewed Snidey, through pursed lips.

"Is you tellings me, Warty Toad is innocent being in alls this mess?"

"Y-y-yes," quaked the slug.

Hobnail could barely believe what she was hearing. "SO, *YOU* DID ALL THIS MESS-MAKING AND BREAKING AND SHELL-SHATTERING, SNIDEY SLUG?"

"*NO!*"

Now their mistress was both confused *and* infuriated. Nobody could access the Dark Hole past Great Boulder and nobody, except for Romany, knew of the secret tunnel. She had left her Dear Ones in safety, by themselves and come back to this devastation! It *had* to be one of them — or both!

"It was the twig-twins!" Snidey managed to peep out at last, his fat, little body trembling. "They're in here with us! Here in the Dark Hole! They climbed over everywhere and wrecked stuff. Warty Toad shouted at them to stop but they thought it was fun! You have to believe me! It wasn't us. It really wasn't us. It wasn't Warty, and it wasn't me!"

Hobnail was astonished at the outburst, but she knew this had to be the truth. Apart from the fact that it was exactly the sort of spiteful, nuisance, bad thing that the Leaf Man's leaflettes *would* do, she had never heard her little pet so indignant and courageous.

She had never heard him stick up for Warty Toad, either.

As if a sudden warm ray of sunshine had struck her, she became filled with love and pride. Thinking hard and replacing the tortoiseshell spike in her cobweb hair, she bent her crooked knees to scoop up her Dear Ones from the floor. "I is believing of you," she whispered, softly. "And I is apology feeling for being a scary, frightening face at you both. Thanks to you, Snidey, for your explanations and loyal feelings towards Warty." Warty Toad felt as if he really would pass out now. Relief washed over him in a flood and he became all floppy in her fingers, panting hard. Snidey Slug let out a thin whistle of air, becoming particularly oozy and rather slippery. Briefly, Hobnail looked around for a sign of the wicked twins, Fiblet and Fibkin, but all that could be seen was the mess — and the slight gap above their heads where Great Boulder had opened up. Their mistress sat down amidst the broken jars and bottles, the bird bits and beetles and cracked sheep bones. And pieces of shiny shell.

"My beauteous shell dish of beauty," she murmured, sadly. "Is shattered being, like my heart."

****

Of course the leaflettes had seen their chance to escape. They had rushed back to tell all.

"She became invisible."

"One minute she was there; the next, she wasn't."

The Leaf Man considered this interesting piece of information. Fiblet and Fibkin waited for his reaction. Liar-nel merely drummed his fingers against the swamp tree. There had to be a reason for this. He knew Hobnail never wanted to be challenged under the long, green, slime fronds and preferred to be left alone, but for her to become invisible somehow was a new thing. There *had* to be a reason.

"And," continued Fiblet, unable to keep his information a moment longer, "she has treasure 'jewellations' in her sea-cave!"

"We have seen the evidence, Liar-nel!" Fibkin corroborated. "She has a golden goblet and a flashy ring!"

"Does she now? That is most interesting, my leaflettes. You have done well to find all this out. You have been trained by a Spymaster! The Moss-makers merely reported something about pitter-patterings of ghostly paws. There was nothing to be seen, they just felt them, and obviously it was nothing to do with old Missus Twelve Fingers. Crow-cus has given up spying at the sea-cave for me because of seagulls, so he is posted on her chimney stack instead. Again, nothing to report. The Mushrumps have told me about some flowers she gathered, but Mr. didn't have a clue what they would be used for, and Mrs. was in a sulk for some reason. I think they'd had a fall-out, so no news from them — but this! This really is *most* interesting." Liar-nel reflected on the information he had received. Why did Hobnail need invisibility? Were there really jewels? A gold goblet and a flashy ring? Really? Without doubt, he trusted the word of his fibber friends as he was the one person they *did* tell the truth to, but how would an old crone like Hobnail get hold of these things? Was she thieving? Was she involved in stolen goods? If so, he could get her into real trouble! That would be excellent! He smiled at the twig-twins. He was developing a lovely, lovely plan to get rid of Hobnail, once and for all. She would be out of the long, green, slime fronds forever!

There were still questions he needed answers to though, so there was nothing for it. He would have to investigate for himself.

****

Quietly, Hobnail cleared up the mess in the Dark Hole. The bird bits were swept up with the glass from broken bottles and precious shell dish pieces. There was no way the dish could be mended. The shell had shattered into shards and slivers so fine that it was an impossible task. The rotting swamp tree bark was scraped from the floor with long, poky fingernails and had to be discarded because it was spoilt with grit and mud. It was easy to collect more, but it took time for the fermenting process to make it as revolting as necessary. The red and black beetles had scurried away, finding safety for the time being in dark corners where they tucked their thin legs into their shiny bodies. Warty Toad would find them again soon enough. The worms and dung flies were nowhere to be seen. The bird songs had long since flown. Only the dead wood lice lay in their dusty, armoured coats, upside down in the dirt.

"Well, my Dear Ones," Hobnail sighed. "The main thing being is this: we is all safe. You boths are withs me and I is withs yous. The nastyful twig-sticks is gone from our Hole of Darkness and we is tidy." She lifted the goblet and placed it on a shelf in the rock to drink from on special occasions or celebrations, whenever they might occur, and admired the ring which was so stubborn to budge past her swollen knuckle. "These two is my new delights. Alls has not been too dreadful being, after alls."

It was just as she was about to suggest they all leave for home, when the wooden door at the bottom of the Forbidden Wall swung open and with a confident swagger, Romany Ratticus, the ruthless rodent, entered. He stood before Hobnail and bowed down low. Snidey Slug glanced at the golden goblet on the shelf and then at the ring on his mistress's finger and felt a bit wibbly in his tummy. He would have rather Hobnail had left those things behind. He wasn't sure how ghost pirates would feel if some of their treasure went missing.

"If I may be so bold," Romany began with a beam. "I would like to declare the arrival of an important visitor!" He scratched a flea. "Someone who would like to make your acquaintance, at last!"

Warty Toad, Snidey Slug and Hobnail all exchanged looks of horror. *An important visitor?* Did this mean what they thought it might? The pirate? The actual *ghost* pirate? Here, in the Dark Hole? Wildly, they looked around them. How quickly could they escape? Was Great Boulder opened up enough? Seeing their alarm, the rat continued hastily. "No! No! There is no need to be troubled. I have expressed to m'lady that you have been most courteous in your welcoming of me into your home. I have described the delicious morsels of good sustenance that have passed my lips. And," he paused, making sure his audience was hanging on his every word, "I have furnished her with a full and detailed explanation of how her map was found and returned by you — for which m'lady is most grateful." Romany was then distracted by another flea which needed a good scratch, giving Hobnail a moment to take this all in. Then, relaxing a little, she gathered her Dear Ones to her and spoke up at last, hoping for the best.

"Is you certain feelings that we is in no danger, sir?"

Romany Ratticus rather liked being called 'sir'. He felt it suited him, for he was certainly no ordinary rat. "Ma'am," he replied, returning the compliment, "trust me. You have nothing to fear. In fact, consider this visit an *honour*."

At these words, Hobnail perked up. An honour! She had never been honoured! She nodded at the rat, who favoured her with his most charming smile.

"So," he continued, "as I was saying, I would like to declare the arrival of a very important visitor!" He stepped to one side. Hobnail, Warty and Snidey's eyes were glued to the tunnel door. "From the battling of waves," Romany announced grandly. "With courage and fortitude. From the depths of the ocean where others' bones drift. From the darkest of nights with only the stars to guide her—"

"*Oh just get on with it!*" thought Warty Toad, desperately, the suspense making him want to wee.

"Please be upstanding for the amazing… the incredible… the magnificent…

MARNIE McPHEE!"

****

The Leaf Man, lurking in the shadows by Great Boulder, heard voices. He strained to listen to every word.

****

Chapter Nine
Pirate

She stood before them at last. The ghost pirate.

She looked proud. Her stubborn chin was turned upwards slightly; her head of dark curls thrown back. Her hands were on her hips, intricate tattoos crawling over them like the tentacles of a miniature octopus and her single, hooped earring dangled and swung as she turned her head slowly to look from Romany to Hobnail, from Hobnail to Warty Toad, and from Warty Toad to Snidey Slug.

Dangle-swing. Dangle-swing.

The laces of her salt encrusted boots were undone and the tongues lolled forwards as if panting for a drink. A black patch was pulled over one eye, in true pirate style, and a pipe peeped out of the top pocket of her swallow-tailed coat. She nodded at Hobnail. Hobnail nodded back, uncertain of how to address a pirate.

"Be you blind?" the visitor queried, looking directly at Hobnail's greyed-out eye.

"Hot coal," Hobnail replied, automatically. "When I is young-being." She looked at the pirate patch. "You?"

"This?" the pirate asked, lifting the patch from her eye. "It just be summat I wear now and then. Makes m' look the part, so to speak." She grinned at the little group before her. "I'd be of a mind t' say 'twere musk shot, but I'd be lyin'. Marnie McPhee always got 'em first!"

Musk shot? Warty Toad felt a bit poorly. He noticed the blade belted at her waist. Snidey slid a little closer to Hobnail and stuck himself stickily to her hairy lower leg. This was all a teensy bit awkward, they both thought. How do you proceed when before you is a pirate — *a ghost pirate* — who had invited herself in?

Do you ask her if she'd like a cup of tea?

No tea in the Dark Hole.

Do you ask her to join you for a bite to eat?

Only some old woodlouse jam remained.

Do you ask her to leave?

I don't think so.

Fortunately, for the two Dear Ones, Hobnail felt no such concern about the niceties of entertainment. She turned and sat on a rock, indicating another one opposite for Marnie McPhee, scooped up Warty Toad, placing him under her armpit for security and plucked Snidey Slug from her leg, popping him behind her ear where he could feel warm, safe and a bit limp. Romany Ratticus sprang onto a jutting out piece of stone in the wall of the Dark Hole and the pirate took her seat.

"I'd better be tellin' you a little about m'self," said the pirate, knocking her pipe against a rock and beginning to pack it with tobacco. "Are ye sittin' comfortably?"

****

Marnie McPhee had been a wilful youngster. She hated all gentle games and preferred to play with the wild, rough boys. Her parents did not understand her and tried in vain to make her wear nice dresses, have nice girls as nice friends and behave modestly, but every moment she could, Marnie would disappear, shouting and spitting and scrapping, coming home late with mud and blood and bruises all over her. Her reputation for being ruthless in fights was equalled by no other — and by the time she was eleven, she had run away to sea.

On hearing this, Hobnail warmed to the pirate stoking her pipe. They had a few things in common, it seemed. As lazy smoke rings spiralled up to Great Boulder's bottom, she remembered how *she* had forged a life for herself in her tumbledown cottage and here, in the Dark Hole under the long, green, slime fronds, to get away from those who did not understand *her*. She knew what it was like to stand up for herself and be fearless. They both wore patches over an eye. They both had a certain way of speaking which was their own style. Rubbing her stooped shoulders with a six-fingered hand, she relaxed. This ghost pirate was more like her than she had expected.

It wasn't long before Marnie had met other 'Ladies and Gentlemen of Fortune', as they called themselves. The docks were full of people wanting work, often loners or petty criminals, some with sailing experience and some with none. Although the work was unlawful, dangerous and difficult, it was accepted eagerly by those who wanted it, with no questions asked. Marnie cropped her hair short and began life on board ship, learning the ropes, tying knots and changing sails as she did so. It suited her well. Life with the crew was tough and harsh, but they all worked with a fierce loyalty, to each other and Captain Conrad Coldblood, determined to succeed and afraid of nothing.

"Ye can't beat the feelin' of a steady breeze in the sails an' the whiff of salt spray in ye face," Marnie announced to her audience. She raised her pipe. "Nor a pipe o' baccy in ye hand an' a jug o' grog at ye feet while the ship is a-rollin' on the waves." She closed her eyes for a moment to take herself back to the days she had loved. How many escapades she had enjoyed with her shipmates: Squire Mulligan, Charlie Crow, Bill the Bosun, Jeannie Laffite, Mad Jack the Coxswain, Bold Bess, Doctor Merrick and Young Pierre, the cabin boy! In time, she made her way up through the ranks to become a true member of the crew, fighting alongside the others, and nothing could quicken her pulse more than the glorious sight of a treasure-laden Spanish galleon on the horizon! All that gold! All those necklaces, bracelets and rings! All those goblets and fine wines! The thrill of the chase! The excitement of the skirmish! The battle! The clash!

And then... the grim satisfaction of a job well done...

It wasn't all skirmishes though. Now and then, land appeared out of the ocean, offering them the chance to restock the ship with fresh food and water, anchor weighed only when pineapples, mangoes, oranges and coconuts were safely stowed. It was always a welcome break and the crew took time to laugh and joke and sing. It was on one of these island trips that Marnie had met Romany. He had jumped into the *Jasmine*

Pearl as she rowed back towards the big ship with her cargo of delicious food.

"D'ye remember that, Romany, eh?"

The rat grinned and nodded. "It was only you, m'lady, who knew I was a Ratticus and not a mouse, as I recall," he chuckled. "The others all called me Enor at first, on account of my size, if you remember…"

Marnie McPhee laughed out loud at this. The two exchanged affectionate glances of understanding at the joke which left Snidey Slug rather puzzled.

"'Course," Marnie continued. "'Twasn't all sea-thievery, fights and fruit. Oft the ship would list to port or starboard an' we'd 'ave to scurry round like ants on the deck to shift the weights of those caskets. Then there'd be the storms. Come at night they would. All lightning strikes and boomin' thunder an' waves; the ship being shook like a wet dog; men pinned to the ratlines."

Snidey Slug was trying his hardest to follow the story but had to interrupt. Feeling emboldened from his safe position behind Hobnail's ear, he piped up, "'Scuse me, but what are ratlines?"

"Allow me to explain," answered Romany with a slight, but important, clearing of the throat. "I rather think this is my area." Marnie smiled, her eyes crinkling in amusement at her pi-rat. "Ratlines are small ropes which act like rungs of a ladder up the rigging, easy for ruthless rats to run up. Some of the sea-farers got pinned to them in storms because the wind was so strong. This meant they couldn't move, so saved their lives, really. They certainly didn't fall overboard!"

134

Once the ship was full of spoils, the mariners made their way back home. Some family members would come rushing at the sight of the sails on the horizon. Charlie Crow, Bill the Bosun, Jeannie Laffite would make their way to the ale houses to spend their wages, whilst Squire Mulligan and Mad Jack would meet villainous acquaintances down dark alleys, to make shady deals. Marnie McPhee rested and then kicked her heels in boredom until the next sailing was due, when the crew would meet up again, with much cheering and back-slapping, ready to face a new adventure.

Snidey had been riveted. His head was full of storms and fights and ships and sea. He had listened with a mixture of terror and admiration. Warty Toad, on the other hand, had a few misgivings. This was all very well, but Marnie McPhee was still a baddie and he felt he had to speak out. "Don't you think what you did was…" he began, hesitantly. He couldn't take his eyes off the dagger at her belt, but because he was such a good, highly principled toad, he just *had* to say it. "Don't you think what you did was… erm… um…" He gulped, making his eyes pop a little. "Was a bit… bad?" Quickly, he ducked under Hobnail's armpit and hoped for the best. The pirate took a long suck at her pipe, not in the least bit concerned.

"Bad?" she repeated. "Bad?"

Warty Toad said nothing more. Marnie threw back her ringlets and hooted with laughter. It echoed in the Dark Hole. Romany chortled to himself and waited for her to answer fully.

"Yes, toad," she agreed, her face suddenly deadpan serious. "'Twere a tad naughty, but 'twere great fun, too! I've 'ad the best life!" And with that, she raised one booted foot to cross it over her leg, leant on her elbow and sang softly:

"I've sailed in many a boat loyal and true,
Over seas and the oceans, so deep and so blue,
Wi' cap'ns and shipmates who loved a rough life,
Who stole from the rich men by dagger and knife!
And it's oh so long ago, and so, so far away,
And I'll sing m' sea shanty forever, they say."

Of course, it had been wrong to live a life like that. Good people, upright people, law-abiding people had nothing to do with the likes of Captain Coldblood and his crew. They were considered vagabonds, scoundrels, cut throats and blaggards. The good people avoided them at all costs, with their hard hearts and pirate ways — but they knew nothing of the friendship and loyalty between them. They knew nothing of their vows of honour and allegiance. These rogues of the sea had found true friends who were like family and made a life for themselves which they loved.

Warty's question did bring Hobnail to her senses, though. What her Dear One had pointed out had been quite right. Much as she had been interested to hear about the wicked life of Marnie McPhee and, having very little music in her life, Hobnail had really enjoyed the sea shanty, the fact remained that Marnie McPhee *was* a pirate. The fact remained that she *was* in the Dark Hole with them and she *had* hidden her treasure in Hobnail's sea-cave. *Her sea-cave!*

137

And worse still, she didn't look as if she was going anywhere.

****

Liar-nel was a bit frustrated. He could not hear as much as he wanted to. He lay face down in the moss, pressing his ear into the slight gap left by Great Boulder. Much of the conversation from the Dark Hole was a little too muffled and he struggled to understand the odd way of talking. However, he had heard bits quite clearly. It was obvious that Hobnail had a visitor. This visitor talked of gold coins and jewels and goblets. Fiblet and Fibkin had told him they had seen a goblet in Hobnail's hand and she had a flashy ring, so she must have got these things from the visitor. He had heard the sea shanty too.

"And stole from the rich men by dagger and knife!"

The Leaf Man smiled to himself. There were definitely stolen goods involved here! He had two choices, now. One, would be to get hold of these precious treasures for himself — and he considered for a moment or two how marvellous he might appear, bedecked in golden finery, jewels on each of his twiggy fingers and necklaces around his leafy neck, drinking water which had dripped and

dropped and

dribbled and

drobbled

from the long, green, slime fronds into shiny goblets. He thought about how fancy he would look with bracelets and brooches and buckled belts adorning his fine stick body and was very tempted. He could call himself *Lord Liar-nel of the Leaf!* His other option though, gave him even more satisfaction. Much as he loved his vision of vanity and wealth, he knew he could get Hobnail into serious trouble now. He knew he could get word to the town that the old crone was storing valuables that she had no right to. He knew this would get rid of Hobnail from his domain. She would be caught and locked up! He had all he needed. He had his information. He just needed to hatch a plan.

****

Hobnail had to speak up now. For a long time, she had worked hard to settle herself and her Dear Ones in the old cottage and Dark Hole. They had made a life for themselves which they enjoyed and the three lived in harmony, each understanding the other, away from the threat of outsiders. This was very important to them. The sea-cave, however, was the most precious place of all. This was only Hobnail's. She was not prepared to share it.

"If I may be questioning of you, Missus Pirate McPhee," she began.

"M' name be Marnie! I'm pretty sure we can be friends, eh? What d'ye think, Romany, eh?"

The pi-rat nodded.

Hobnail began again. "If I may be questioning of you, Marnie, why is you hiding your pretties in my sea-cave? I is

139

aware-being that you is wanting to safe-keeps them, as Romany has explainerated, but is you of understanding that it is *my* sea-cave? I is not wanting visitor pretties — or visitors — therein being!"

Marnie McPhee looked curiously at the hunched woman in front of her. Hobnail was much older than she, and with her hunched back and blind eye, she looked strangely witch-like. She wondered about her life and her need for solitude. "I 'ave to keep 'em," Marnie explained. "I 'ave to keep 'em safe. I can't join m' maties wi'out 'em. Me and m' rattie thought the cave was ideal."

"Well, is not so ideal being!" Hobnail replied firmly, looking rather haughty. "I is not happy-feeling about them being there."

Marnie knocked the smoky contents from her pipe onto the floor of the Dark Hole, thinking hard. "I 'ave a better idea," she announced. "I can bring m' pretties 'ere! No one'll find 'em through the labyrinth of tunnels. This dark 'ole be an even better 'iding place, methinks!" She looked Hobnail straight in the eye and began to sing again:

"My pretties are hidden in yonder dark cave
Cos, I promised m' maties their treasure I'd save,
But what do I do now? I'm out of my mind —
As I can't take 'em wi' me, or leave 'em behind.
And it's oh so long ago - and before you I stand
Wi' a weight on m' shoulders; m' heart in m' 'and."

Hobnail looked back at the pirate. She knew Marnie was asking for her help. It was all very tricky. She didn't want the pirate treasures in the Dark Hole, but it *was* better than the sea-cave. There wasn't much space here, in between the Forbidden Wall and her rocky ledges and shelves, but at least it *would* get Marnie McPhee out of her cave. Her greyed-out eye began to plot and plan. There *had* to be a solution to suit them all. After a moment, Hobnail spoke. "Well," she declared, with a slapping together of her six-fingered hands indicating there was work to be done. "We'd best be move-shifting your pretties then, hadn't we? Warty? Snidey? I is needing of your assistance, if you please so. And Romany Ratticus, I is needing of yours, too." She would get the pirate's booty transferred to the Dark Hole and go from there. Her blind eye had the beginnings of a plan.

Her inner eye was waking up, though. Her inner, forward looking eye could see that something else was about to happen, if Hobnail wasn't very careful.

****

Chapter Ten
Hiding Places

Liar-nel had heard from Crow-cus. His bird-spy, bored with circling around Hobnail's chimney stack, had flown off to the cave once more, ready to do battle with the seagulls, if necessary. He had not seen anything much, but he had heard echoing voices from within the rocks and a sort of dragging sound as if heavy items were being pushed and pulled. Once, he thought he had seen footprints in the sand outside the cave, but there appeared to be nobody there to make them, and the ripples of waves soon washed them away. He dismissed them as shady shifts of light, or stones, momentarily exposed by the movement of water. He knew something was happening, though. Hobnail and others were definitely back at the sea-cave and *something* was going on. Crow-cus thought this was enough to report to the Leaf-Man — and Liar-nel was certainly very interested.

"The Mushrumps have not told me she has been seen under the long, green, slime fronds," he mused, petting Fiblet and Fibkin who lay snoozing in his lap. "And the Moss-makers are quiet; no clacking message has reached my ears. So how is she getting to the sea-cave? Is she using her invisibility trick to disappear again?" He paused to consider.

142

"Tell me Crow-cus, what of the slug and toad? Have you evidence of their whereabouts?" The black crow thought carefully for a moment. Had he heard their voices echoing? Had he heard them squabbling like they did under the long, green, slime fronds when Hobnail was collecting?

"Because," continued Liar-nel, drumming his stick insect fingers. "If they are around, there must be another way through to the cave. As far as I know, the precious pets can't hide themselves in the same way as she does and if they haven't been seen, there must be another route!"

Crow-cus put his head on one side, stared at the Leaf Man and then he nodded, his powerful beak hooking down low. Yes, he had heard their voices. The slug and the toad *were* with her. And he thought he had heard the scurrying of rat's feet, which had made his mouth water.

****

Hobnail's inner eye was not happy. It was uneasy and tried to send Hobnail warning messages about future events. It could see Liar-nel clearly, near to Great Boulder. It tried to foretell his plans, concentrating hard, advising Hobnail, but she wasn't paying attention. *Listen to me! Listen to me!*

Crates and boxes and caskets were being dragged through tunnels, with muscles straining and panting breath making foggy puffs in the damp air. It was hard to move them because most of the passageways were too low for Hobnail and Marnie to stand upright, and so the pretties had to be lugged behind,

143

or pushed in front. It was very difficult to be bent over, pulling and shoving as they were, and they grunted and groaned with effort. Now and then their heads hit a rock on the roof of the passageway, making them yell out in annoyance and stop, to give the sore place a good rub. Romany, ever important, had nominated himself 'Relocation Executive-in-Chief' and had taken charge of the removal proceedings, shouting orders whilst standing on a sea-cave rock, tail in hand. Warty Toad and Snidey Slug took up the rear, calling out if any of the jewels or coins fell from the boxes as they bumped over the stony ground. All in all, it was not a very quiet business and Hobnail just hoped that they were far enough underground for their voices not to carry. She did not realise the echoes had already alerted a certain black crow and given him the information Liar-nel needed. As soon as the first crates were placed in the Dark Hole, they all returned through the door at the bottom of the Forbidden Wall, traipsing along the tunnels to the cave once more.

"This is being wearisome work, I is thinking," grumbled Hobnail, grabbing one of the final boxes. "I wills be happy-faced to think my sea-cave is empty again times, but I is exceptional tired feeling and woulds be liking of a cup of primrose tea."

Marnie looked at her strange new friend. "Primrose tea?" she queried. "*Primrose tea?* Why, I be of a mind to help m'self t' some good grog! You can join me and m'rattie, if ye like!"

"I is not sure feeling that grog is pleasant tasting or of good health giving, thanks you very much," Hobnail replied a

144

little stiffly. She was quite sure that fresh primrose tea, taking flowers from the spring fields surrounding her cottage, would be very much better for her than some ancient mariner's strange liquor. "Is kind being of you, though," she added, not wishing to sound ungrateful. "I'll sticks to my flower tea, if you please so."

Her inner eye flashed another note of caution to Hobnail and this time managed to stop her in her tracks, temporarily. She closed her good eye to concentrate, but it was hard with all the fuss around her. She couldn't really make out what the warning was, and so shook her head to clear it and carried on.

****

The Leaf Man was indeed at the entrance to the Dark Hole. Great Boulder was having a little shut-eye and had not noticed. The plan was to get hold of some of the treasure which he was sure Hobnail was storing, to show as evidence. If he didn't have evidence, it would be very difficult to convince people in the town that the strange, old crone who lived in the tumbledown cottage on the edge of the forest had stolen goods in her possession. Fiblet and Fibkin were at his side, as always; his loyal helpers.

"We must be quick and cunning, my leaflettes," whispered Liar-nel, through the dripping gloom. "We must be cunning and quick! We must get into this Dark Hole and seize the proof we need, make our escape without her knowing, then dash to the town and raise the alarm. I'm pretty sure the police will be very interested in all this!" The twig-twins nodded. They winked at each other, ever ready for fun. They looked at sleepy Great Boulder.

"How will we get past big boulder bottom, though?"

"It's certainly squidged over the entrance."

"Squidgy, squidgy. Eeeeuw."

"It's too fat to roll."

"Fatty fat, fat."

"It's too fat to push."

"Squidgy, squidgy, fatty, fat."

"It's too sleepy to help."

"It wouldn't want to, though, would it?"

Liar-nel put a twiggy finger to his grinning lips and shushed them. "Just watch the Master of Masquerades at work," he sniggered. Then, assuming a very *different* voice he cried, "GREAT BOULDER! BE OF WAKING IN NATURE! I IS NEEDING TO GO INTO MY DARK HOLE AND I IS NOT HAPPY YOU IS IN MY WAY!" Lazily, Great Boulder stirred. "MOVE YOURSELF, IF YOU PLEASE SO!"

Without any hesitation, and not awake enough to look around itself properly, the huge boulder rocked backwards and forwards, slowly building up enough momentum to move away from the entrance to the Dark Hole. It never thought for a moment that it wasn't Hobnail giving the command. As soon as there was a big enough gap, Fiblet and Fibkin leapt from their hiding place and twizzled into the Dark Hole for the second time in just a couple of days. They remembered how they had caused havoc the last time they were there, and it

146

made them chuckle and chortle to think of the mess: broken jars and containers, scattered ribs and bones, lost beetles — and, of course, the precious shell dish. Shattered. Fiblet and Fibkin's fabulous fun! Liar-nel slithered from his swamp tree hidey-hole and, with a flurry of falling leaves and a clattering of sticks, joined them.

"Well, well," he smirked, looking around him. "I knew it! You were right, my little friends, and Crow-cus was right, and I was right. Ho-Ho! Hobnail *is* hiding stolen goods in here! Ho-ho! She's going to be in a whole *heap* of trouble now! She has been thieving *and* smuggling. Somehow, she has got this loot and sneaky-snorkily moved it from the sea-cave to here, hidden from prying eyes! We must get the word out!" Fiblet and Fibkin hooted with laughter. "Now, let me see… which of these beautiful trinkets should I take as proof?" The three intruders proceeded to ransack the boxes and crates and caskets which had been stacked so carefully in the Dark Hole. Necklaces, bracelets and jewels fell through their wicked twig fingers as they grabbed and grasped and grappled.

Great Boulder blinked. Slowly, stupidly, it came to its senses.

Blink. Blink.

Hang on a minute! *That wasn't Hobnail's voice!* The huge rock struggled to rouse itself as it began to realise what was happening. There below it, in the Dark Hole, which it had to guard, day-in, day-out, were impostors! *OH NO!* Great Boulder knew only too well what its punishment would be if Hobnail found out it had let them in. Not only would it be

147

spiked with her tortoiseshell barb, but also there was a real risk of being zapped with electrical fingers, and… and… and… it might possibly be reduced to a small seaside pebble, to live the rest of its days being tossed about on the seashore by relentless bashings of waves! Oh the shame! *DO SOMETHING!* With an enormous boulder-grumble and a grinding of rock, it began to move. The opening above the tricksters began to close up and the dim light which shone upon them began to disappear. Fiblet and Fibkin realised immediately.

"Whoa up there, Big Bottom!" Fiblet yelled.

"Not so quick, Fat Face!" Fibkin shrieked.

"GET SCRAMBLING OUT OF HERE, FAST!" yelped the Leaf Man.

Leaving the precious finds behind them, needing hands free for the escape, the three jumped and span and twirled through the air, up towards the ever-decreasing gap over their heads. The twiglets were out first, and both thrust helping stick hands to drag Liar-nel to safety, scuffing and grazing his thin body as he squeezed through the remaining crack.

With a resounding thud, Great Boulder closed up and breathed a great sigh of relief. It shuddered violently, sending tremors through the rock, then it assumed an air of nonchalance as best it could. Now, to pretend the whole thing just *hadn't* happened.

****

"How long do you think we have to stay here, Mrs. Mushrump?"

"Hard to say, Mr. Mushrump. Hard to say."

"We have to wait though. Wait and see where she goes, don't we? I say, don't we, Mrs. Mushrump? Because Liar-nel told us to."

"That's true, Mr. Mushrump. That's true, but it's hard to say how long."

"An hour? Two? What do you think, Mrs. Mushrump?"

"An hour, maybe, Mr. Mushrump. Maybe two. Like I say, it's hard to say. You know how it is when we're on guard."

"Yes, Mrs. Mushrump. I know that."

"Well, why ask, then, Mr. Mushrump? Why ask when it's so hard to say?"

"I'm getting cramp, Mrs. Mushrump."

****

With a final heave, the last of the cases of pretties was pushed through the door at the bottom of the Forbidden Wall and Hobnail collapsed in a heap. Marnie McPhee followed, clutching her pipe and a flagon of grog, with Warty Toad, Snidey Slug and Romany, behind. Hobnail shut her good eye and took a moment to recover and pretend she wasn't involved with either a ghost pirate or a phantom rat. How did she get herself into this?

"M' pretties are so pretty!" announced Marnie, dancing around the Dark Hole in glee. "Look at 'em, see? So shiny and

149

gold and gleamin'." She let some doubloons spill through her fingers and dangled a necklace in the air. "I 'ave m' daggers and m' goblets! M' coins and m' rings! What d'ye think, Romany? Aren't they shiny and gold and gleamin'?"

"Romany Ratticus, the ruthless rodent, has to agree, m'lady," agreed the pi-rat. "Extremely shiny and gold and gleaming." And he smoothed his ratty whiskers with a thin paw.

Hobnail sighed. Time to look at her Dark Hole and see exactly how much room, all of this had taken up. As soon as she looked though, her eye widened in horror. What a mess! She hadn't left the boxes and crates and caskets like this, all opened and spilled! Why were the pretties scattered all over the floor? Marnie hadn't noticed, or if she had, she didn't care, such was her delight in being surrounded with shiny, gold, gleaming treasure. Hobnail raised a grimy hand in the air. "Be hushed in your excited feelings, Missus Pirate McPhee!" she exclaimed. "We has been visitors having in my Dark Hole and this is bad-nasty news for us!"

The pirate froze, the necklace in her grip swinging silent seconds like a clock pendulum. Romany's whiskers drooped a little as his paw covered his mouth. Oh. Heck.

"This has the makings of our twig-twins about it," declared Hobnail, knowing how Fibkin and Fiblet worked. "I is knowing it isn't any of us looting and rooting and messing about. We has been all busy kept, in our pretties movement from the sea-cave." Warty Toad and Snidey Slug were very relieved their mistress did not think it was anything to do with them, this time. "But, my dearies," continued Hobnail, "what dids they want? Is they just nosy-being or is they up to mischief-making, I wonders?" Then a frown cloud crossed her face. "And," she began to mutter, threateningly, "how dids they get in here?"

Hobnail scowled up at Great Boulder... and slowly retrieved the tortoiseshell spike from her hair...

****

Liar-nel was sore. His stick legs and arms were scraped. His leaf skin was dishevelled. He was also very, very frustrated.

"I can't let this opportunity pass," he hissed into the dripping drops of the long, green, slime fronds, to nobody in particular. "She has valuables which don't belong to her. I want to get at them to prove she is a thief." He twirled a stem of greenery between his fingers as he thought.

"I have to get into the Dark Hole again. I will *not* give up." He knew he would have to wait for the Mushrumps to inform him. He had them in position, fat fungi sitting next to Great Boulder. They were so slow with their news, though! Or the Moss-makers. They could spread the word more quickly. *Clack! Clack! Clack!* They would let him know Hobnail's movements.

And then he could make his.

****

151

Marnie McPhee decided she was unfazed. She had dealt with worse than the likes of a leafy stick insect and some tricky twigs. When she was told about them, she threw back her ringlets and roared with laughter. "I'll slash 'em t' ribbons, m' maties!" she avowed. "I 'ave m' faithful dagger, ye know!"

Romany joined in, eager for a fight. "Romany Ratticus, the ruthless rodent, is by your side, m'lady! Only dogs show fear!"

"And then we can stay 'ere, Romany," Marnie replied, gesturing around the Dark Hole. "We can stay 'ere wi' m' pretties, all as safe as a caged parrot, comin' and goin' t' the sea as we please! We 'ave the best secret hidin' place 'ere. The tunnel is 'idden and the *Jasmine Pearl* will wait on the waves for us t' sail when it pleases us. I 'ave a new lease of life!"

Hobnail was suddenly horrified. Stay here with the pretties? Come and go as she pleased? Use her tunnel to reach the sea-cave whenever she liked? Speechless, she watched as the pirate sat back comfortably on a rock and pulled out the cork from the flagon of grog with her teeth. Romany scratched a couple of fleas, scrambled onto Marnie's lap, and settled himself down to sleep.

"I'll keep all the pretties in this 'ere dark 'ole,
And no one will know when I come and I go.
So, take up your flagons and raise me a toast
To m' rat and m' maties and to bein' a ghost!
And we're oh so happy, m' dear rattie and me —
Oh, how bold and how clever is Marnie McPhee?"

****

Chapter Eleven
Spell

Enough was enough!

Hobnail knew she had to do something. The pirate ghost and pi-rat really could not live in the Dark Hole with their pretties. They were unwanted visitors, not invited guests — and there was not enough space. Moving them out of the sea-cave was good, but they were still where she did not want them, and her planning eye had been plotting to work out a solution. Taking advantage of a short time when Marnie McPhee and Romany had ghosted off somewhere, Hobnail rummaged through books on the Forbidden Wall. They were covered with the usual, dusty cobwebs and her searching had disturbed all manner of nasty hurry-scurryings, which had delighted Warty Toad. He took advantage of the situation with enthusiasm, the plump spiders bursting in his mouth, all squirty juices. Page after page was turned in Hobnail's grubby hands. There were so many instructions and ideas here: incantations and recipes, hints and tips, chants and charms. The *Spell of Invisibility* was written in a scrawling hand, but she needed something more.

"What are you looking for, Mistress?" squeaked Snidey Slug. "Can I help? Warty Toad is obviously no use because he's too busy stuffing his face."

Warty swallowed a rather large spider and belched.

"'Tis a bit tricksy, my Dear One," replied Hobnail, a bent finger crabbing its way down a list of ingredients. "I is needing a tweak to my invisibilising. Wolfsbane in snakeskin is all very well being, but I is in needs of an extra layer of vanishment."

"An extra layer?" repeated Snidey.

"Yes, dearie."

"Of vanishment?"

"Yes, dearie."

"But it worked fine, last time," persisted the puzzled slug. "And why do you want to invisibilise again?"

Hobnail was too distracted to answer. She had found the extra ingredient, listed right there in front of her, as a variation to the spell. Her grey, whiskery eyebrows knitted together in a frown. This item wasn't easy to collect, unfortunately, and she didn't have much time. If necessary, she would have to think of a substitute and hope for the best. After all, the snakeskin had worked when it should have been lizard skin, so for this item, perhaps she could use something else that was similar. Slamming the great book shut, her plan clear, she made her way out of the Dark Hole to gather whatever she could, under the drips and

drops and

dribbles and

drobbles of the long, green, slime fronds.

****

"She's collecting again, Mrs. Mushrump."

"That she is, Mr. Mushrump. That she is."

"What is it she's after now, Mrs. Mushrump?"

"Hard to say, Mr. Mushrump. Hard to say."

"But can you get a good look, Mrs. Mushrump? Can you get a good look? We'll have to let Liar-nel know, you know."

"I know we'll have to let him know, Mr. Mushrump. I know we'll have to let him know. Trouble is, it's hard to say, so I can't say what I don't know, if you know what I'm saying."

The Mushrumps needn't have worried. They were always late with their news and the Moss-makers had beaten them to it. *Clack! Clack! Clack!* The Leaf Man had already been told. Instructing his leaflettes to stay in safety by the swamp tree this time, Liar-nel unstuck himself from the bark and made his way stealthily, back to the Dark Hole.

****

Marnie McPhee had reappeared. She sat, with Romany, on her favourite rock, enjoying the effect of the glow worms' light which danced over her pretties. Hobnail had also returned and was busying herself with her large copper pot. Warty Toad and Snidey Slug knew all the signs that went with copper pottery and decided to take cover, knowing how unnerving it could be.

155

Eventually, their mistress cleared her throat and addressed the pirate. "Excuse me, Missus Pirate McPhee, if you please so."

"You are excused," Marnie grinned, throwing back her dark curls and gesturing around her with a tattooed hand. "Where is it ye'd like to be goin'?"

Hobnail scowled as Romany Ratticus chortled. "*I* is not wishing to be going anywheres," she retorted. "It is you and your gentleman rat who wills be going and we is needing to be quick-stickery about it."

Marnie sighed. She thought she had made herself quite clear. It was impossible for her to go. She was stuck here, in limbo. She was not leaving the pirate treasure. She could not leave the pirate treasure. She jutted out her chin stubbornly and looked up at Great Boulder. This ghost was going nowhere.

Hobnail saw this reaction and pressed on. "You and Romany must be leaving our home places. You and Romany has been in my sea-cave and the Dark Hole — Romany has been eating of eggsies in my cottage-home, too! I has been helping of you and now is true times for you to be going." She paused for a minute, wondering how to explain. "I is hoping my plan will work, although it is new in nature to me. I has special powers, you understands. I learns these from very small being. I is of mind thinking that I cans send you both to join your crew." Another pause. "With your pretties."

The pirate lowered her gaze to regard her new friend, the strange old crone, with sudden interest. Now, Hobnail had her full attention. Join the crew? Her shipmates? *With* the treasure? She leaned forwards, her elbow on one knee, fist under her chin. Her eyes met Hobnail's good one and they looked steadily at each other. "How's that then?"

"You will needs to be trusting of me," responded Hobnail. "I cans do this, I is thinking, although I don't have quite the right requirements about me. I is hoping for the best."

"Well, Romany? What d'ye think, eh?" questioned Marnie, addressing her loyal rat. "What d'ye reckon? Is it worth a try? D'ye reckon we could do this, wi' a fair wind and a bit of sailor's luck, m' matie?"

Romany jumped off the rock to look at her, squarely. Turning his head slightly, he considered Hobnail who was standing in the middle of the Dark Hole, six-fingered hands held out at either side, beseechingly. He looked for Warty Toad and then Snidey Slug, but they were out of sight. Marnie's questions hung in the air. Eventually, after weighing it all up, the pi-rat spoke. "Romany Ratticus, the ruthless rodent, has thought about this," he announced, drawing himself up in an important manner. "Romany Ratticus, the ruthless rodent, reminds you, with all due respect, m'lady, not to forget that we are a courageous couple! A tremendous team! A daring duo! We have faced many adventures together and we have always been triumphant! We have *never* shied away from any situation of uncertainty. We have been through thick and thin — er stuff." The pi-rat broke off to gather his thoughts, then holding up a thin paw to reveal his four ratty claws in turn, continued. "I have considered the options, and these are as follows, m'lady:

157

❖ Número uno (first claw): We could stay here. We like Hobnail, Warty and Snidey. The food's good. We are safe.

❖ Número dos (second claw): We could try to take our treasure and live as ghosts elsewhere, since Hobnail is not keen on us staying. But I don't know where. Or how.

❖ Número tres (third claw): We could leave the treasure here, give up our ghost lives and go to our shipmates. But we have made a pirate's promise. It would be broken. We would not have any mates left to go to.

❖ Número cuatro (fourth and final claw): We give Hobnail's plan a try. It might not work, but there's a chance it might. Who knows? What I *do* know is we are a courageous couple! A tremendous team! A daring duo!"

Romany finished his little speech with a flourish of his scrawny paw and Marnie McPhee broke into applause. "You've been countin' those Spanish doubloons again!" she laughed.

"In short," the pi-rat added, solemnly. "I am by your side, m'lady."

Hobnail's craggy face was serious as she listened. Her inner eye was sending hot warnings to her and this time she heard them loud and clear. "Time is sun-dialling fast," she murmured. "We must act speedily and chip-choppery. We has someone returning to our Dark Hole — and be sure, he is not a friend-face." She stood before the pirate ghost. "Is you ready and willing to try my plan?"

Marnie regarded Hobnail carefully, then looked fondly at her devoted rat and thought about her choices. For as long as she could remember now, all she had wanted, was to be with the crew and to reunite them with their treasure. She nodded slowly as rare tears began to well up in her eyes. "M' rattie's been m' comfort, but I 'ave to say, I miss m' maties. If we could both join 'em, it'd be a wonderful thing. I *could* take m' pretties wi' me, couldn't I?" She looked earnestly at Hobnail. "So, we could all be together, like in the old days?"

"I wills be trying of my best," came the reply. "We all wants the same thing to be happening, I is thinking."

In truth, Hobnail knew this was the tricky part. Her ability to make herself disappear could be transferred easily to others. Whether it would work with *things* like pirate pretties, depended on the final ingredient according to her special book; the ingredient which had proved so difficult to find. *And* the disappearance would have to be *forever.* She closed her good eye to ask her future-telling eye a question: Would sticky tree resin work when it should be watery tree sap? She had not been able to extract sap and so she was hoping for the best. She knew time was running out before she would be in *real* trouble.

Lizards and snakes; resin and sap. All the same, wasn't it?

****

The Leaf Man was waiting.

He had arrived at Great Boulder but had kept himself hidden, hoping for a chance to enter the Dark Hole once more.

159

He knew he wouldn't be able to fool the boulder twice, no matter how good his impression of Hobnail was, and so he had to sit tight and wait. All he needed was the opportunity to get some of those valuables. He didn't care if Hobnail was innocent in all this. He didn't care if he was in the wrong. This situation gave him the prospect of getting rid of her. He was good at lying and deceit. All he had to do was to wait for his chance. His moment.

****

Hobnail had all she needed, more or less. The copper pot had been lifted onto the fire rocks and the flames had been lit by a zapping of her sixth fingers. With care, she selected a jar from the Forbidden Wall and shook five stems of purple flowers into the pot. The seeds of wolfsbane scattered as she did so, heating and spitting. Smoke began to fill the air. The trimmed off remains of the snakeskin were thrown in.

"Great Boulder!" she cried. "I is needing some air down here, if you please so. Be open-upping a little to let this smoky burn smell leave us."

As Great Boulder heaved itself to and fro to open up a gap, Hobnail indicated where Marnie McPhee should stand, with Romany perched on her shoulder, the pretties surrounding her buckled and booted feet. She looked brave and proud. Her lace-trimmed shirt was open at the neck, the tie hanging loose. Her right hand rested on her dagger which was sheathed in her belt, and her pipe was tucked in the pocket of her swallow-tailed coat. She stayed stock-still, in position. She was ready to leave.

A darkness passed over Hobnail's face as she crouched down low on the floor of the Dark Hole. She began to rock and to mutter. She clenched her knuckles, making them crack. This had to work! For everyone's sake. Quickly, quickly, now!

"Seeds of wolfsbane, skin of snake,
Join together, majik make —
Jewels and pretties, caskets, gold,
Rings from fingers ... dead and cold.
Mariners, two, should not be here,
Take them — make them disappear!"

There was a light skittering behind her, which disturbed the moment. Hobnail halted her incantation, abruptly. She froze. A scratchy sound came from the other side of the Dark Hole.

A scratchy sound like a stick on the ground.

And then there was a leaf rustle.

Slowly, Hobnail turned, fearing who she might see.

"HO-HO!"

The dreaded Leaf Man, Hobnail's foe, stood before them! He grinned at her as he took in the scene. He saw the pretties and the copper pot. He saw Marnie and Romany, waiting.

"Well, my ugly little petal," he snickered. "How lovely to catch you at home. I just thought I'd pop in to see you but, my my, what is *this*? What *are* you up to?" He took a step forwards, his legs stretching taut, ready to spring. His sinister smile never faltered; his twiggy fingers were flexed, ready to grab. "Nothing to say, my sweet?" he smirked. "Well, let me tell you what *I* think you are up to. *I* think you have items of value here. Items which do not belong to you. *I* think you are about to try to squirrel them away from prying eyes, but these peepers of mine have spotted you in the act and I'm going to have to take some from you!"

Hobnail stayed silent. She knew better than to enter into conversation with Liar-nel. She begged her greyed-out eye to guide her. *The resin!* It reminded her. *Don't forget the resin!* She reached into the pocket of her old overcoat. The Leaf Man crept towards her, one creepy step-at-a-time. "*I* think you ought to just step out of my way and allow me to—"

There was a sudden *clatter!*

With a defiant roar, Marnie McPhee leapt over the pretties in one long, booted bound, dropping Romany amongst them. She had heard enough. Hobnail's plan would have to wait.

"AVAST YE!" she bellowed. "BATTEN DOWN YE HATCHES EVERYONE! THIS LANDLUBBER IS ABOUT TO BE FISH FOOD!"

And brandishing her dagger she lunged at the Leaf Man, cutting swathes through the smoky air of the Dark Hole. Liar-nel ducked swiftly and retreated, his locust-like legs springing and bouncing to keep him safe. Marnie advanced, her eyes glittering, her trusty dagger stabbing and plunging and thrusting forwards. Romany dusted himself down speedily and dashed to her side. "I'll go round the back, m'lady!" he shouted. "A two-pronged attack to save our booty! Let's make him shark bait!"

Shaking with fear, Hobnail pulled a small bottle out of her pocket and unstoppered it with her teeth, pirate-like, herself. The sticky resin glooped its way into the copper pot and began to sizzle as she cried out in desperation:

"Not just invisible, merely unseen —
Send them to where they should have been!"

She clapped her hands and gritted her yellow teeth. This *had* to work! She *had* to save them and send them on their way!

It wasn't working, though.

The resin was *not* the right ingredient. Marnie McPhee and her loyal rodent had *not* disappeared. They were still in pitch battle with the Leaf Man, and the pretties were still scattered around.

"Stay back strange pirate person and pesky rat!" Liar-nel was warning. "I have minions who will come to my rescue, you know! I am in control of this place under the long, green, slime fronds and I will fight to the death!" He slashed out with his stick arms and jabbed with his twig fingers, trying to poke Marnie in her eyes. "I will tell the people of all this! I will tell them about your treasure!"

"DEAD MEN TELL NO LIES!" yelled the pirate ghost.

"AND YOU WON'T KILL US!" screeched Romany. "WE'RE ALREADY DEAD! SAVVY?"

This momentarily took the Leaf Man aback. Dead? How so? Whatever did this fleabag mean? He hesitated for a crucial second — which was his undoing. With an unexpected swipe of her dagger and a splintering *crack* of dry wood, Marnie

McPhee hacked off Liar-nel's left hand and sent it flying! Tree sap spurted into the air from his arm branch. *Tree sap!* The fountain sprayed over the Dark Hole. It sprayed over Hobnail. It sprayed over the pirate and the pi-rat.

It sprayed right into the copper pot!

There was a tremendous *BANG!* The Dark Hole shook.

Hobnail fell to the ground in a heap.

****

Chapter Twelve
Gifts

A dagger remained on the floor of the Dark Hole.

A dagger with a well-used blade, now dripping with tree sap.

The Leaf Man was nowhere to be seen.

Hobnail crawled over to it, picked it up and turned it over in her hands. Without doubt, it was a weapon of great age and had seen much action. How many fights had this dagger fought? How many victims had it slain? How many times had

Marnie McPhee brandished it in her piracy? Hobnail shuddered. What a dreadful thing it was. She did not want to keep it; it represented violence and combat. She had to get rid of it. She looked around.

The pirate was gone.

The pi-rat was gone.

The pretties were gone, apart from the jewelled ring, safely on her finger, and the goblet she had taken as rent. Warty Toad and Snidey Slug could not be seen, but she knew that they were still hiding. "All's well being, my dearies," Hobnail called out, a little shakily. "Liar-nel has left, taking his hand with him. Our visitors has left, also. I is hoping that they is with their maties and is having a grog party, with sing-songing and such like." She put on her shabby overcoat and tucked the dagger into a pocket. "I has a little job to do, Dear Ones. Is not dangerous but is needful to be done. You tidies up for me after the copper pottery ands I wills meets you back at the cottage. We wills be together again in no times." So saying, Hobnail climbed the dug-out steps which led up to Great Boulder and squeezed herself out through the gap. She planned to make her way to the sea-cave by striding confidently through the long, green, slime fronds to the forest edge. No secret tunnel today. She didn't care that the Leaf Man's spies would see her and report her movements. She *wanted* him to know her movements. She wanted him to know that she would do as she liked, go *wherever* she wanted to go, *whenever* she wanted to, and *nobody* was going to stop her! She would collect her trusty, bent bicycle from the edge of the forest where it had been left when collecting wolfsbane, and wheel-cycle her way to the cliffs, enjoying the rush of wind in her face, blowing away her troubles — and the cobwebs — from the Dark Hole.

****

The Mushrumps had seen her, of course. They had seen her black boots stomping their way through the Leaf Man's territory, but by the time they had got their message to Liar-nel, he already knew. The Moss-makers, *clack-clack-clack,* had already felt, and reported, the thunder of her feet as she squashed their busy knitting — *clack-clack-oof!* Crow-cus had already spotted her arriving at the edge of the forest and picking her bicycle up from the grass. He had followed her past Badgers' Bank and over spring-flowered fields where the noble sheep munched, until she reached the cliffs. He told Liar-nel how she had thrown her bicycle to the ground and clambered down to the rocky beach. He had circled on salty sea air, watching her as she waded out to the sea-cave and disappeared inside.

But, the Leaf Man did not want to know.

The Leaf Man was no longer interested.

The Leaf Man did not care.

He hooked his legs around a swamp tree and nursed the stump of his left arm, tree sap still weeping from it. It ached and ached, and each throb reminded him of what had happened. He was embarrassed that he had failed. He was furious his plan had not worked. He was appalled that he had actually *helped* Hobnail with her spell. He felt sick with shame.

****

The hens were enjoying the spring sunshine when Warty Toad and Snidey Slug returned to the comfort of Hobnail's tumbledown cottage. They were stretching their wings, flapping and fluttering. They were clucking contentedly as they pecked in the grit. Some were basking amongst the late daffodils; others dustbathed in a warm corner, scrunching and shaking their feathers, happy with their hen thoughts. The two Dear Ones found a shady spot and settled down to wait for Hobnail. Lucy-fur, sunning herself as usual, paused for a moment in her fur-licking, to acknowledge their return. She looked around briefly to check for rats, but there were none. She sniffed the air to make certain, but all she could smell were bluebells, so she resumed her ginger grooming and took no further interest.

"A lot seems to have happened in the last few days," commented Warty. "I'm rather pleased everything is back to normal at last and we can relax again. No more pirates. No more pi-rats. No more ghosts." He yawned as his poppy eyes began to droop. "And I don't think the Leaf Man will pester us for a while, so all's well that ends well, whatever that means." He sighed as he shuffled into a comfortable position, ready for a good, long snooze. All the excitement had been quite exhausting.

Snidey looked at his dozy friend. He could see that Warty was almost asleep. Snidey, however, was not sleepy. He smiled craftily and slid a little closer so he could just whisper into the toad's ear hole. "Yes," he murmured. "We're fine… as long as the twig-twins keep away, that is." He paused for a second, then added, "You never quite know when they're going to turn up, do you?"

Warty awoke with a jump, instantly feeling sick at the thought. Fiblet and Fibkin could be anywhere. Any of those sticks on the ground could be them. Actually, there were lots and lots of leafy twigs, once you started to take notice of them. Uneasily, he looked around, blinking and swallowing. "You don't think they're here now, do you?" he gabbled, nervously. "You don't think they're ready to make trouble again, do you?" He gulped. "Can you see them, Snidey? Should we hide again?"

Then he saw the slug's smirk.

Snidey was laughing quietly, his squishy grey sides wobbling with mirth. He wibbled and wobbled, chortling and chuckling. He was very pleased with his little trick. Warty Toad scowled at him. "Well, thank you very much!" he groused. "You really didn't have to remind me about them, did you? I'm not going to sleep *now*, am I?"

"Suit yourself," replied Snidey, most amused. "Just saying."

****

The dagger was flung high into the air above Hobnail's head. It spiralled, glinting and flashing in the sunlight before splashing into the water. Gone. Hobnail, sitting on a rock, smiled a yellow-toothed smile. It felt good to be rid of it. She gazed out to sea and drew a deep breath through her flared nostrils. She had done well. She had made two new friends and learnt a lot about their lives. She had helped the two lost souls keep their promise, had come through the whole adventure unscathed, *and* — a sudden grin lit up her face — Liar-nel had been chopped like firewood! Ripples of seawater ran over Hobnail's boots as she dangled her feet. She sploshed them up and down, enjoying the sound and the sight of splattering sea drops. She felt like she did when she was a child and had first found this place.

Safe.

And then, as she sat, remembering all that had happened, faint voices came to her ears. Faint, singing voices. The sound of them dipped and bobbed, sometimes soft, sometimes loud; ebbing and fading one second, then rushing towards her on the crest of a wave, the next. She turned her head to one side so that she could listen more carefully and immediately recognised the tune of the pirate's sea shanty.

"Goodbye, fare thee well now, our time 'ere is done,
We've met with our maties an' we're all 'avin' fun!
Wi' grog in our flagons, we've no more t' fret
But the friends we are leavin', we'll never forget.
And we're oh so 'appy — and so, so far away —
And we'll drink t' your health now, forever they say!"

Delighted, Hobnail touched her hairy lips with the six fingers of her right hand and blew two kisses over the sea.

The sun was beginning to set, and it cast orange glimmers onto the waves. Her sea-cave was becoming more shadowy, but a little light still reached inside the entrance, catching Hobnail's eye. It paint-brushed a tiny, stone shelf. It was a tiny, stone shelf which was never used and so was always overlooked. Something was glittering on that tiny, stone shelf. It shone in the orange glow. Curious, she clambered off the rock, straightened her bent back and went to investigate.

There, lying on its side, not forgotten, but left, was an exquisite, jewelled dish, inlaid with gold and blood-red rubies.

A pirate's present.

A true treasure.

171

Trembling slightly, Hobnail reached out and took it from the tiny, stone shelf. She walked slowly out of the cave and resumed her seat on the rock, placing the beautiful dish in her lap. She had never seen anything so wonderful. Her heart swelled with happiness and a rare feeling of contentment. She would find a very special place to keep this. Somewhere very secret. Somewhere away from prying eyes and spiteful thoughts. Somewhere only *she* knew about.

"I is grateful feeling to you Missus Pirate McPhee," Hobnail whispered hoarsely out to the sea. "I has never been given of presents and this dish is being even more perfect than my one of shell. I will cherish-love it, always. Thanking you, Marnie."

As if in reply, a piece of flotsam appeared, bobbing on the surface of the water. Gentle ripples floated it towards Hobnail, until it washed up against her rock.

It was one last gift.

It was a piece of driftwood.

It was the name of a boat.

"The Jasmine Pearl."

****